The Girl I Love

W0259558

Happy Reading!

Amit Nangia

The Girl I Love

AMIT NANGIA

Srishti
PUBLISHERS & DISTRIBUTORS

Srishti Publishers & Distributors
Registered Office: N-16, C.R. Park
New Delhi – 110 019
Corporate Office: 212A, Peacock Lane
Shahpur Jat, New Delhi – 110 049
editorial@srishtipublishers.com

First published by
Srishti Publishers & Distributors in 2018

Copyright © Amit Nangia, 2018

10 9 8 7 6 5 4 3 2

This is a work of fiction. The characters, places, organisations and events described in this book are either a work of the author's imagination or have been used fictitiously. Any resemblance to people, living or dead, places, events, communities or organisations is purely coincidental.

The author asserts the moral right to be identified as the author of this work.

All rights reserved. No part of this publication may be reproduced, stored in a retrieval system, or transmitted, in any form or by any means, electronic, mechanical, photocopying, recording or otherwise, without the prior written permission of the Publishers.

Printed and bound in India

To Arpita,

The girl I love.

Acknowledgements

Foremost, I need to thank you Arpita, for motivating me to follow my passion of writing. I hope you can feel the bits and pieces of us together in this book and smile. Thank you for letting me share a bit of us with the world. I love you more than my life itself. I always have... I always will. Thanks a lot for supporting me in this journey.

Deepest gratitude for my family, for endless encouragement and unconditional love. To my brother, Anuj, for always challenging me to be true to myself, and to my sister-in-law Parul, for believing in me. Thank you so much for your unwavering support. I wouldn't be able to do what I love if not for both of you.

Jayanta Kumar Bose sir – A million thanks for a million things. For being the one to believe in me, for your ideas, for the counselling, for listening to me and for letting me write my heart out.

A huge thanks to Arup Bose! Thank you for coming up with brilliant ideas for the book, the promotion and providing so much support, encouragement and enthusiasm. Thank you for taking the time to read this book several times and providing valuable feedback.

To my editor, Stuti Sharma, who found the writer in me. Thank you for your keen insight and for keeping me on track. And for doing it all with a big smile. I don't know how you do it. Thank you for editing my book and making me feel like it's going to be something special. Your pride in me really means a lot.

Special thank you to Sandhya Sridhar for her insights in helping me refine my work.

Publishing a book is a group effort. I'm lucky to have the support of an entire team of incredible people at Srishti Publishers, a truly groundbreaking publishing house.

Thank you Kairav and Myra – you know who you are! Thanks for sharing your love story which inspired me to write this book. Hope your entrepreneurship start-up reaches the heights you want it to reach.

Saving the best for last – my nephews, Vidit and Savir. Thank you for loving me, for your innocence, for telling me interesting stories of your day at school, even when I looked like I had crawled out of a cave, and giving me the energy back to do what I love.

The mobile always rang when she was least expecting it. It also always managed to alarm her beyond measure. The shrill, loud sound could have woken up the dead. Myra woke up sweating. It was as if a never-ending nightmare was clinging to her; her heart was thumping as a response to the sudden stimuli. She blinked into the darkness, wondering what time it was, and subconsciously cursed the caller.

She peered around in the dark. She couldn't see a damn thing. She knew it was late, really late.

She also knew that *he* always called at late hours. The dead of the night was the time that this hidden side of him emerged. She had known him for too long to know that in broad daylight, he was way too confident and full of himself to bother about small things. She knew his all-time companion too well, his ego, which he wore like a raincoat to save himself from being drenched by the heavy droplets of doubts, questions and pain. It was only in the dark, late at night, when his ego slipped into a slumber, that the devils he tried so hard to hide broke free, to emerge and taunt him. And that's when he usually called.

"Myra Sharma, my angel in disguise," he would say.

She smiled gloomily and squinted at the alarm clock by her bed.

"Not at this hour, dude! Even the spirits are fast asleep. You can just put those devils to rest all on your own, because your angel is not coming out there tonight. Not this time. No way. Not at all. For god's sake, it's four-thirty in the morning Kairav!" Groaning, she stared at the clock in disbelief.

Four-thirty!

She realized she had been talking to herself.

She managed to slither out of her blanket and grab the mobile without knocking over the stack of books lying on the edge of the table.

"Kairav."

She dropped her head back on her pillow, eyes closed, the mobile tucked between her ear and her shoulder.

There was a pause, then a familiar husky male chuckle. "How the hell did you know it's me?"

"Who else calls me in the middle of the night?" she mumbled sleepily. "You broke up, didn't you? Your *second, big, break-up!*"

She realized she had emphasized the three words more than was necessary. A long pause again. She heard him release a tensely-held breath that conveyed his pain and regret and who-knew-what-else.

"Yeah! Yeah, I did." His voice was soft, but rough. "How did you know?"

"Come on, Kairav! I know you very well, I could see it coming!"

He chuckled, but she could hear the effort it took him. Then he sighed again and she could hear the faint sound of his hand rubbing against his unshaven face.

She could imagine him sitting there in the dim room, the lights switched off, staring into the darkness, one hand holding a glass full of whisky with ice, the moist droplets on the outside of the glass reflecting the dampness of his eyes. He must be telling himself he didn't care, that he was over Tanya, the feelings had died six months ago when he started avoiding her by travelling more than he usually did, and keeping away from her and other such nonsense. He must be thinking that he had known it all along and this was just the sentence declaration, that he could handle it. That, hell, it was the second time after all, and he was an old hand at it. That he was too indifferent; too damned cool to feel anything but relief that it was finally over. That he was free.

But she knew him well. The soreness would be there, even if unacknowledged. It ran too deep, was too complicated, for it not to hurt. Even the second time around. And so, much later, he'd have sat there in the infinite emptiness of his huge house, listening to the murmur of the air-conditioner and the sound of his own heart. All alone. And would have felt the loneliness and the memories close in on him. And then, finally, he'd have reached for the phone, afraid of the devils winning against him.

She squeezed her eyes closed. She was not going to give in this time and drive all the way out there just to hold his hand and tell him that she was sorry it hadn't worked out, and that everything would be all right soon. Not this time. Not anymore.

"How about putting on some decent clothes and coming out?" he asked quietly. "We'll pour ourselves a drink and toast the old times."

"It's four-thirty in the morning, Kairav," Myra said through gritted teeth.

She was not going, damn it!

"And you sound as though you've been toasting old times half the night already, and my share as well, yeah? Now just put that sick cap back on the bottle of your Blenders Pride whisky sitting on the table beside you. And listen, one more evil thing, please! Just burn that picture of Tanya that you're holding in your hand and flush the ashes in the toilet. Remember the movie *Jab We Met* that we were watching the other day? You thought the 'burn-your-girlfriend-and-flush-her' idea superb? Now do it yourself and I am sure you will feel very good. Go to bed, Kairav! I am sure it will help. We'll talk in the office in the morning, okay?"

"Damn!" He laughed softly, the husky, honey-warm sound wrapping around her like a web. "You scare me sometimes, lady. But you're only half-right; it's a bottle of twelve-year-old Johnnie Walker Black Label Scotch on the table beside me, not Blenders Pride."

In spite of herself, Myra had to smile. "Well, I'm glad to hear that you're handling things with a little class this time, Kairav. When Ria broke up with you, you got drunk on cheap whisky, threw up five or six times and were hung over for three days. This is progress."

"Yeah, well, I guess you get better at some things if you do them often enough," he said quietly. "God knows why, but I can't seem to get the hang of staying in a relationship for too long. But let's look at the brighter side, I'm getting pretty good at the break-up part. What say?"

"Oh, Kairav..." She could feel his misery right through the phone and fought to ignore it. She had to stop running to him every time he called.

"Myra?" It was a whisper filled with pain. "Myra, damn it! I need you."

She gritted her teeth and shut her eyes so tight, they hurt. She knew this process so well, having gone through it over and over again. Every molecule of her was trying to resist the sweet pull of his voice, yet again, without use.

"I have to be at work in five hours, you know that partner!"

He laughed that low, teasing laugh he knew she couldn't resist. "Come on, Myra! Don't be so stubborn to your buddy. What's the worst thing your partner is gonna do to you – kick you out?"

"I should be so lucky," she shot back furiously.

Another laugh, gently compelling. His magic was all but taking over her reason.

"Lighten up a little, Myra. Take the day off. How does that sound, huh?"

"And who's going to finish that report we need for our meeting with Kapil Kapoor tomorrow afternoon?"

Kairav moaned. "Cancel the meeting. Hell, cancel tomorrow. I'll give myself the day off too, and we'll go do something that we have not done for long. How about going on a trek? You haven't gone on a trek with me in over a year."

"Get serious, Kairav," Myra chanted in a monotonous, robotic voice, which she knew would get through to him. "Getting a chance to get investment from Info Capital comes along once in a lifetime. Just imagine what our growth path would be after this – the exponential growth in turnover, our dream of expanding the firm to a global footprint! UrbanFork will move into a different league once we receive the kind of funding we are hoping to get. Are you trying to tell me that just the thought of pulling off an impossible task like that doesn't make your little entrepreneurial heart beat faster?"

"Okay, okay! No day off for either of us." He gave a discontented sigh. "So, why don't you bring your stuff over here with you and you can go to work with me?" He laughed softly. "And Myra, having known you for so long, I know you're not going to get any more sleep anyway. Why lie awake in your bed thinking of my misery when you can be here and ease my pain?"

Myra lay staring at the ceiling in the darkness, telling herself for the hundredth time that she was absolutely *not* going to drag herself out of bed and go all the way out there. No, never! Not this time, under any circumstances. She imagined the bed grabbing at her, and the doors of the house shutting automatically to stop her from going; yet Kairav's teasing words were making it impossible for her to stay.

No, she had to stop doing this. She was turning over a new leaf. Was giving the old Myra Sharma a version upgrade and introducing a new 2.0 improved version – one who was impermeable to sweet-talking men with hazel eyes and enticing smiles.

"Did it ever occur to you that I might not be alone?" She glared at the ceiling. "That I just might have better things to do at four-thirty in the morning than help you toast your ex-girlfriends goodbye? I'm a *normal* twenty-eight-year-old single woman, Kairav. I do have a life other than being your partner in UrbanFork during the day and helping you deal with break-ups in the dead of the night."

"We promised once that we would always be there for each other. Remember?" he murmured. She knew he was modulating his voice to get her to be there. She so knew it, and wished she could tell him that she could see through him now. "Not going to break a promise to your best friend, are you? Not going to leave your best friend alone when he needs you so much?" he wheedled.

Unthinkingly, unintentionally, she ran her finger along her right thumb, feeling the crest of a scar. It had been twenty years; things had changed, but the scar had stayed. Had become more prominent, getting deeper and more prominent, like their friendship.

Best friends. Yes.

Then, realizing what she was doing – what he was doing – she slapped her open palm down onto the bed, eyes narrowed to slits.

"Damn you," she whispered furiously. "Damn you, Kairav. That's so not fair!"

He did not say a word, and Myra went on, "I've always been there for you when you've needed me. All you've ever had to do was call and—"

There! She had done it again; and this time by herself. He didn't have to say anything; he was smart enough to let the silence speak for him.

Myra closed her eyes and blew out a long breath, swearing softly at him.

A husky, warm laugh came from his end, enveloping her like a hug. She opened her eyes and swallowed a sigh, wondering who she'd been trying to kid, telling herself that she'd be able to resist him. She never had. Not once in twenty-three years.

"An hour," she muttered. "And put the cap on that damned Scotch, because if you're all drunk and over-emotional when I get there, I swear I'll turn around and come home."

He laughed. "When was the last time you saw me over-emotional, darling?"

"Six years ago, when we went through this the first time," she reminded him testily. "And put on the coffee maker."

"Black coffee?"

"Super strong." She sat up and rubbed her eyes. "You owe me for this, Kairav. You owe me big time! Don't think I will let you go for ruining my sleep like this, and that too for the nth time in life. I hate you!"

"Name it and it's yours, darling," he said with deep-throated laughter. "Love you too, girl."

And the most terrible part of it was – considering those few precious moments it took him to say the words – he probably meant them.

It didn't take her long to reach his place. All she had to do was to pull on her comfortable old jeans, wear a top, shove her hairbrush and Mac make-up kit into her handbag, pull out some suitable clothes for work the next day, and that's about it. Heading for the door grabbing her slim leather Kipling bag while fumbling for her car keys, she left her home at an unearthly hour for Kairav. Once again.

She had to be out of her mind. Yawning and shivering slightly with the cold, Myra unlocked her red Honda Amaze and slipped behind the wheel. She so knew she was a fool. Shaking her head in disgust, she put the key in the ignition and turned it.

"What did you think, Ms. Myra Sharma? You thought that you have this under control now? After all these years? You are not a kid anymore. It was one thing to fall in love with the sweet guy next door when you were ten; quite another when you are just two weeks shy of your twenty-ninth birthday...and he still doesn't have a clue how you feel about him!" This time, the voice in her head was pretty loud. She shook the thoughts away and returned to cussing.

Pathetic, that's what it was, she told herself grumpily. Just damned pathetic!

It took her about twenty-five minutes to get to his house. The usually crowded road was wondrously empty. The streetlights were making the roads shine and the cool wind caressed her cheeks ever so lightly.

It always gave her an odd feeling, driving up the entrance lane to his apartment, with its overhanging trees, the air heavy with the scent of wet earth from last night's heavy rain. The first time she'd come up here was nearly twelve years ago, and the memories of that night were still fresh.

Kairav had been a twenty-two-year-old college senior when she'd left the college – brilliant, popular and full of dreams. He, along with his two friends, Sharad and Vineet, had been talking of quitting college and starting their own venture. These had not been just some random dreams, because not long after Myra had left, they'd done it. And just about fifteen months later, their small three-man company had become one of the fastest-growing start-ups in Delhi, its three young owners successful beyond their dreams and wealthier than any had ever imagined possible in this lifetime. The app that they had created for integrating gyms across the country, selling subscriptions so that customers could use gyms wherever they were, had been a runaway hit. But that had been a lifetime ago, and Kairav had coasted highs and lows. Highs when they had hit big time and lows, when Sharad and Vineet had done a googly, twisting a spin-off of the idea and starting their own company, leaving Kairav bitter and cheated. He had never understood why his two friends had done this to him. Along with it came the realization that mere friendship was not enough; trust was important.

Myra, at that time, had moved back home to Kanpur, had been working in a bank, her first job after college, and was bored and restless. Her job was interesting, but not challenging enough. She needed something else to satisfy her drive for achievement.

That's when Kairav called her out of the blue, offering that she join him in his new venture, UrbanFork. He had offered her a 30% stake in the company, and proposed that she hold the financials, along with the back end. That too, seemed like a lifetime ago, with UrbanFork creating waves and making a mark in the restaurant and dining space.

Now here she was. Again.

Myra smiled grimly as she made her way towards the visitors' parking area of the apartments in Greater Kailash II. The building rose dark and solid against the night sky, the front entrance lit up like a special Diwali decoration created especially for her arrival. There had been no such lights to welcome her on that night twelve years ago; the night that had changed her life in so many ways.

It had been late that night when she'd gotten here, nearly midnight. She'd come back to Delhi from Kanpur because she couldn't stay away any longer. She had decided, finally, that she was simply going to have to take the initiative and make him fall in love with her, starting out with a full-fledged seduction she'd planned down to the last detail.

She hadn't called or written to warn him that she was coming, wanting to surprise him, wanting to see the look on his face when he opened the door and saw her standing there, suitcase in one hand and a bottle of sparkling wine in the other.

Well, she'd surprised him all right! Perhaps, shocked him! He'd pulled the door open and stared blankly at her for a full five seconds. He had then frowned and asked her what the hell she was doing here at that hour of the night.

Then, as if recovering, he'd laughed and wrapped her in a long, warm hug. He'd barely placed the bottle of the sparkling wine on the bar and had told her to sit down, when a huffy female voice had called his name from the depths of the house. Before Myra could gather her shocked wits together and leave with some measure of self-respect still intact, a tall, slender hottie had drifted into the living room, tangled and sleepy-eyed.

She'd been wearing a satin negligee and nothing else, and had gazed at Myra with extreme displeasure.

And then Kairav, grinning like a fool, had come back into the living room, put his arm around the creature and kissed her. While Myra was letting it all sink in, one by one, his foolish grin was now accompanied by some foolish words. "This is Ria, my girlfriend. We have been living-in for about six months now."

Live-in relationship!

Deep breath in; deep breath out. Wasn't that how dad had said you could overcome anxiety?

Even now, more than twelve years later, Myra felt a wave of chill brush her cheeks. Now, much later, she could think of a hundred things that she could have said; all the anger and restlessness could have been thrown right back at him, just like his foolish smile. But back then, embarrassed and angry, she'd muttered something in response, and had dashed right out of the house with her suitcase and the wine bottle, her tears stinging her eyes as much as the 'hottie' had stung her heart.

Kairav had come after her asking her what the hell was wrong and why she couldn't stay at least long enough to tell him what she was doing in Delhi and where she was going to stay. But then Ria had called him back to her and Myra had fled into the night, stumbling into a hotel at one in the morning to cry her eyes out, heart-broken.

If she'd had enough money, she'd have been on the next plane back to good old Kanpur. But she'd had too little cash and way too much pride. In the end, she had talked herself into rebelliously staying in Delhi, finding a good job and a nice apartment and even a couple of boyfriends. And to hell with Kairav and his live-in girlfriend.

That had been twelve years and two almost-Mrs. Kairavs ago; and today, she was still here. Myra mentally patted her own back for being able to fake such a brave front all this while, as she brought the car to a stop in a parking space for guests in front of his apartment block. To think of it, everything had worked out so wonderfully smooth on the surface. She loved her work, had a nice and comfortable home, a city full of great friends, and the cherry on the cake was that she had finally found a man who loved her and wanted to marry her. Everything was seemingly just so perfect; except for that one thing she still wanted most of all – Kairav.

Myra took the elevator to his apartment. He'd left the door half open for her, and as she stepped into the dark stillness of the foyer, she paused on an impulse for a second or two, listening. But there was no hint of unfamiliar female perfume in the air, no tinkle of female laughter, no husky voices calling out to him, no him.

Grinning at her own silliness, she confidently walked through the darkness into the corridor leading to his living room, instinctively avoiding the table on her left and the fancy stand with the super expensive and beautiful flower vase on her right. It was so like a second home up here, everything as familiar and comfortable as old friends, a part of her, because they were all a part of Kairav. She breathed deeply, loving the male scent of the cologne he always wore.

The living room was dark. The only illumination came from the street light throwing a glow through the curtains of the living room. She could see Kairav sitting in the rocking lazy boy couch, back in the shadows, head dropped back, eyes closed, one foot on the edge of the centre table, a perfect picture of a modern-day *Devdas*.

There was a bottle of Scotch beside his other foot on the Kashmiri carpet, open, almost half gone. A half-empty glass sat on the glass table near his right hand. Giving all this company, was a box with half-a-pizza and a plate with remains of pasta, on the floor around him.

She stood there for a moment simply looking at him, wondering at the charm he held for her even without doing anything at all. At the same time, she felt his pain inside her, as sharply as if she was experiencing it. Snapping out of it in a bid to get things under quick control, she slipped off her jacket and hung it over the nearest chair. She walked around to right behind him, reaching down to gently massage his shoulders.

He gave a groan of delight and smiled, not opening his eyes but relaxing visibly. "My angel of mercy! I didn't know if you'd come today."

"You knew damned well I would come, Kairav!" She told him directly. "I always do."

"True." He reached up and caught her left hand in his, pulling it down and kissing her palm. "I don't know what I'd do without you, darling. You're the only thing that makes sense in my world half the time. And by god, the only person I can count on."

"Best friends, remember?" Myra said it lightly, as she walked around the chair to sit facing him on the floor, her fingers still meshed with his. He looked tired and slightly fatigued in the dim light, the lines on his face darkening with every effort at smiling. She could see that his smile was only half-hearted, that too, probably the best he could come up with in her presence.

"You look like hell, Kairav. Since when have you been sitting on this couch drinking, to celebrate your new-found freedom?"

Kairav had to smile. Opening his eyes, he turned his head to look at her, liking, as always, what he saw.

Even at five in the morning, in jeans and a sweater and without a hint of make-up, she looked perfect – skin glowing, locks of thick black hair spilling around her shoulders, clumsily brushed, yet lustrous. But that was Myra, always calm and peaceful and in control, never letting things get to her. Not even a jackass who was her best friend.

"I have been on this couch for three days, I think…" His neck was stiff and he massaged it wearily. "Or maybe four, I can't remember."

"Ah, the Scotch and the fast food diet," Myra said sarcastically. "I have an idea! Maybe I can find some '*tere bin main yun kaise jiya*' type music in my car and you can sing along with it. That would be fun."

"I am glad you came over," Kairav muttered, wishing his head would stop thumping. "I love it when you get all supportive and sympathetic like this." He stretched out his other hand, reaching out for hers.

"Hey, you better love me enough, you know. I'm here, am I not?" She gave him a high-five on the stretched hand. "How many other people do you know who'd get out of a warm bed at four-thirty in the morning to come over here and listen to your moans and groans?"

"I'm not moaning and groaning," Kairav said through gritted teeth. "I'm celebrating! Every man has the right to celebrate a little when he gets rid of a woman who had been binding him. I'm a free man again. If that's not reason to celebrate, I don't know what is." Except that he didn't feel like celebrating, Kairav thought. He felt like sliding deep into an endless hole and sleeping. Sleeping for about two months straight without anyone disturbing him. Or maybe…just Myra.

"Oh, Kairav." Her voice was just a murmur, and he felt the touch of her fingertips on his cheek. Then her arms slipped gently around his neck and she knelt in front of him, holding him tight. Kairav found himself hugging her back, with his face nestled in her neck, breathing in the warm, female scent of her as if it were a healing ointment.

"Kairav, I'm sorry it didn't work out. I really am," she murmured. "I know you'd hoped it would this time. That everything would be perfect."

Kairav smiled remorsefully. "I'll live, darling. And I feel like a damned fool, dragging you over here. When I read the papers this morning I figured, hey, I'm cool. It's over and done with, and it's what we both wanted. It's not like it was some big surprise or anything. Then…" He shrugged, and kissed the side of her throat.

She in turn rubbed his back to ease his pain a bit; she knew what he would be thinking, how he would be trying to tell himself that all is well.

"I don't know. I just sort of gave up, I guess. Don't ask me why. It's not as though I loved her or anything."

"You did, once," Myra said softly, pulling back gently to look at him.

"Did I?" Kairav heard the resentment in his own voice.

"Well, you must have thought you did. Same thing. That's what you always say."

"I've been sitting here for hours, trying to remember just what the hell it was that I felt for her. There must have been something. I mean, a guy doesn't start living with a girl without feeling something, right?"

He looked at Myra seriously. "It scares me a little sometimes. This is the second time, Myra. I can live with one break-up, but now again! When it was Ria, I thought that all one needed to keep two people together was stunning sex."

He managed a brief smile, as much at Myra's expression as at the memories.

"But when I got in a relationship with Tanya, I thought it was going to be forever. I thought I knew what I was doing. That what we had was something that would last." Another smile, slightly sour this time. "A year later and she is gone. And I still don't know what the hell went wrong. It just…faded. I remember waking up one morning, looking at her lying beside me and wishing I'd never met her."

"But the sex was stunning." Myra tried to cheer him up, winking.

Kairav had to smile. "Oh, yeah! The sex was stunning. Right up till the very end."

Myra's look held his for a second too long; then she looked away quickly, colouring ever so slightly, and stood up. "I'll, umm, make you some breakfast. I hope you've put the coffeemaker on, like I told you to."

"Yeah, yeah!" Kairav nodded absently, watching her as she started gathering up the food leftovers around his chair. "Yeah, the coffeemaker is on." Remembering with sudden unexpected brightness, of what it had been like with Myra.

One weekend of heaven, that's how he'd always thought back on it. Three days of a kind of closeness with Myra that he'd never experienced before or after. It was supposed to have been a getaway weekend to Shimla. Just the four of them – Myra and her boyfriend, he and Aditi. Just that Myra and her boyfriend had broken up two days before they were supposed to leave. Kairav had said there was no reason why she shouldn't still go, considering that the arrangements were all in place. Aditi had exploded, shouting something about three being a crowd just before she stormed out, doors slamming behind her back.

But they had stuck to the plan, at least half of it. He and Myra, both suffering from the "love-gone-wrong" syndrome, had gone all by themselves. The Queen of Hill Stations had done what neither of them had ever expected. They'd come together like fuel and flame and even now, twelve years later, he could feel his body swirl slightly with just the memories of it.

It had been a magical weekend. But then they'd gotten back to Delhi and college and somehow – he never was sure exactly why – the magic had vanished in the hustle and bustle of everyday life. Aditi had come back apologetic, and it had been Myra's turn to go storming off in a flurry of doors slamming.

He'd gotten all that sorted out about the time that college had let out, and Myra had headed down to Bangalore to take a summer internship with her brother's IT firm.

He'd planned to go after her and talk things out. But he and his two college buddies, Sharad and Vineet, started playing around with a new idea that would integrate gym usage and would sell memberships, and did not realize when summer went by. When Myra came back, things were stiff, seemingly overformal and awkward between them. And then, out of the blue, she'd decided to move back to Kanpur to take up a job in a bank and they'd all but lost touch with each other for almost a year.

There was a beep from the coffee maker, and Kairav blinked, impatiently shaking himself free of the memories.

Kairav looked at Tanya's picture on the wall dispassionately. Strange to think it was over that easily. One year of great sex and a few good times, and then abruptly, he was single again.

It made him laugh for some reason, although god knows it wasn't even funny. Still grinning, he stood up and stretched his arms. Myra was nowhere to be seen but he could hear her in the kitchen. Suddenly, he felt hungry. He picked up the bottle of Scotch and capped it tightly. He then grabbed the half-empty glass and moved towards the kitchen.

She was looking for a coffee mug in the cabinets. Kairav paused by the kitchen door to watch her, enjoying the play of soft denim across the rounded contours of her trim little bottom. That was one thing he didn't see enough of these days. Having Myra as his partner had been smart in a lot of ways, but it also meant that she spent most of her time with him dressed in business suits and smart office wear. Which was a damned shame, he found himself suddenly thinking. A real damned shame!

He set the glass on the counter, quietly walked up to her and slipped both arms around her to nuzzle the side of her throat.

"You know what I was just thinking?" he purred against her ear.

"I'm afraid to ask," she managed to say, just about to drop the coffee mugs she had taken out.

"I was just thinking that we could take the day off. The Info Capital meeting can wait a day or two...I will speak to Kapil Kapoor..."

Her skin was slightly salty, and Kairav nuzzled his cheeks against the lobe of her ear. She gave a tiny start. He wondered why he'd never done this before. Hell, it wasn't as though the idea hadn't occurred to him now and again. But it just never seemed, well, right, somehow, making a pass at your best friend.

"Kairav!" There was a hint of alarm in her voice.

"I have another idea, too," he whispered softly, running one hand gently up under her sweater and settling his palm on warm, bare flesh, caressing her gently.

"Kairav..." She'd stiffened at the first touch of his hand on her abdomen, as though not entirely believing what he was doing.

"We could spend some time together at home," he murmured, slipping the fingers of his left hand under the waistband of her jeans, while letting his right glide up lightly to reach her breasts through silk and lace.

They were warm and full. He remembered how sensitive they'd been all those years ago, how she'd groaned softly when he'd—

"Kairav...!" Breathless with surprise, she recoiled back against him.

"God, you feel good," he growled, filling his hands with the incredible softness and warmth of her. "I'd forgotten how good you feel, Myra." Nuzzling her throat, he spread his fingers across her belly and pulled her against him, pressing gently against her, already fully aroused.

"Remember what it was like that weekend up at Shimla?"

He felt her breath catch ever so slightly and smiled, running his fingertips along the edge of her bra.

"We could have that kind of magic again, Myra. We could—"

"Kairav, wh-what are you doing?" Her voice was an astonished whisper.

"What the hell do you think I'm doing?" he asked with a low chuckle. "It's been a while, but I think it's called foreplay..."

He thought about what it had been like, making love to Myra that first time, wild and vital and so hungry for each other, they'd practically gone up in smoke. Twelve years later, and he could remember that first long silken slide into heaven as though it had happened no more than an hour ago. He could still recall clearly the soft noise she'd made deep in her throat, the way her body had taken him, welcomed him, loved him as he'd pressed deep, deep; slaking himself in the hot, satin depths of her.

Kairav groaned and moved against her and he could hear her moan very softly.

She grabbed his wrist and he felt her fingers tighten convulsively. He remembered what it had been like with her twelve years ago, how she'd gasped with pleasure the first time. He remembered other things too, touching her for the very first time, fingers seeking, finding, teasing. The way she'd pressed her thighs together, embarrassed and a little uncertain, until finally, she'd been fire and honey and hot silken need, and in no time at all she'd arched against his hand, eyes wide with shock and delight.

The knot in his belly tightened thinking back about it, and he moved against her again, pressing himself against her round, denim-clad bottom, feeling his own breath catch. He slipped the metal button on her waistband free and tugged the zipper down impatiently.

"Myra, I want you..." he groaned, moving persuasively against her.

"Kairav!" The word was little more than a gasp. "P-p-please!"

Growling something, he drew his hand from her and turned her in his arms, pressing her back against the wall, one thigh pressing between hers even as he slipped his fingers into her hair. Tipping her face up, he brought his mouth down over hers. And then, very suddenly, she moved her mouth away and turned her face so he couldn't kiss her again, planting both hands on his shoulders and pushing him firmly away.

"Damn it, Kairav, what the hell do you think you're doing?"

"Kissing you," he muttered, trying to do it again. "Damn it, Myra, quit turning away and—"

"Stop it!" she shouted and her shrill voice brought him back to his senses.

She was stronger than he would have guessed and she pushed him back roughly, panting for breath, cheeks blushing, eyes snapping. Shaking her head to get her tangled hair out of her eyes, she glared up at him. "Back off!"

"Myra, for the love of—!" Swearing, he took a step back, blood hammering in his temples; he was so aroused it hurt just to stand there, breathing hard. "What's wrong? What the hell is—?"

"I am not some vacant pair of hips you can just use when the mood strikes you, mister! If you need to reaffirm your manhood or drown your sorrows or celebrate your new-found bachelor status or whatever the hell it is you're doing, fine – but *not. with. me!*"

"What?" Kairav just stared down at her, mind spinning with confusion. "Honey, that's not what—"

"No!" Mouth tight with fury, she glowered right back at him, wrenching the gaping fly of her jeans closed. "Is that why you called me over here tonight? Because you're feeling a little sorry for yourself and figure all you need to get over the break-up blues is a good—"

"Don't even say it," he growled, moving his fingers through his hair. "Look, I—" Swearing violently, he moved away and planted his hands on the edge of the counter, letting his head droop, eyes closed. "I'm sorry," he muttered finally. "Damn it, Myra, I'm sorry. I don't know what…" He shook his head.

And he didn't know, he realized miserably. Sure, now and again he'd thought about what it would be like to make love to her again, but this was more out of alcohol and frustration than any real sense of desire. She was Myra, for god's sake.

His best friend. And you don't hit on your best friend!

"I'm sorry, too," she said finally, sounding submissive. "It was... Let's just forget it, okay? It's five-thirty in the morning, I'm tired. And you're a little too drunk..."

Her small hand settled warmly on his shoulder. "You're my best friend, Kairav. That doesn't mean I won't punch your lights out if you try something like this again, but let's not make a big deal out of it, okay?" She leaned close and kissed him lightly on the cheek. She knew she had to be insane to forgive him for all his crazy mistakes; but she knew it was out of her love for him.

"Go, take a shower...a cold shower! I'll make some breakfast."

He smiled down at her, wondering what he'd ever done to deserve a girl like this in his life. Even at an arm's length, she was the best thing that had ever happened to him.

"If I'd had any damn sense at all, I'd have proposed to you twelve years ago, instead of Ria," he said half-seriously.

She hesitated for just a split second, an odd expression crossing her face. Then she smiled hastily.

"And ruin a perfectly good friendship, Kairav? We nearly did that by sleeping with each other that weekend up at Shimla. Remember?"

"Oh, I remember," he said with a growl.

"And if you remember all of it, we agreed that our friendship was more important than sex. And that—"

"Stunning sex," he corrected straight-faced. "We did agree it was pretty stunning sex, Myra."

"Yes, alright, stunning sex." She was trying not to laugh. "But we agreed that good friends are harder to find than lovers, remember? Even good lovers."

"Great lovers, even," he agreed mildly.

"Great?" She looked pleasantly surprised. "You really thought I was—?" She caught herself abruptly.

Shrugging off-handedly she stepped past him, avoiding his eyes. "Go take a shower, Kairav."

"Yes, ma'am." Grinning, he headed for the kitchen door. "And yeah, you were great. Once we got past all the virginal inhibitions, darling, you were—"

"Censor that," she said quickly, and suddenly started rifling through the refrigerator. "Eggs, bread… How about bread and scrambled eggs for breakfast?"

"I'm easy."

"I've noticed *that*."

"Feel free to take advantage of it."

"Ha! You wish."

Sometimes, Kairav found himself thinking, glancing at her with an unexpected twinge of wistfulness, *Sometimes, I do wish, darling*. But he couldn't say it aloud, of course. Not to his best friend.

Staying there, setting the glass-topped table in the big verandah off the kitchen, making bread and scrambled eggs, pouring orange juice, felt like the hardest thing Myra had ever done. At first, she had decided to leave at once. But her love for Kairav had made her stay put where she was – right next to him when he needed her.

Every instinct she had was telling her to run. To hide. To shut herself up in her apartment and pull the bedsheet over her head and simply die of humiliation.

One touch, that's all it had taken. One touch and she'd all but melted in his arms like an overheated chocolate brownie, as flexible and eager as a silly teenager. Where she'd found the strength to push him away, she'd never know.

Because she hadn't wanted to. All she'd wanted was for him to strip her out of her jeans and ease her down onto the floor and make love to her as though his very life depended on it.

Holding a handful of tangled hair off her forehead, she took a deep breath and wet her lips, closing her eyes for a reassuring minute. It was all right. She could handle this.

The secret was to stay cool and simply pretend it had meant nothing. Nothing at all.

Kairav was drunk, so totally drunk that he wouldn't remember a thing some time later. He'd been hurt, vulnerable, off balance – all unknown emotions to a man who prided himself on his practical, logical and level-headed approach towards life.

She'd been there, warm and feminine and reassuringly familiar. His best friend, his confidante, the one person who probably knew him better than anyone else did. What was more normal than to reach for her, seeking to put his world right again through the comforting rituals of lovemaking?

The odds were that he wouldn't even remember the incident in a day or two.

So no harm had been done.

As long as she kept the whole incident in perspective, she reminded herself gloomily, as long as she didn't try to delude herself into believing that Kairav, with blinding insight that had eluded him for twelve years, had suddenly recognized that she was the only woman for him.

Feeling herself more in control of the situation, she added a few spices and onions to the eggs, then started beating them with a wire whisk. It was time, she told herself calmly. In three weeks, she was going to be twenty-nine years old. Too old to still believe in miracles. It was time she shook herself free of Kairav once and for all, and got on with her life, because she would be damned if she was going to turn into one of those silly women who waits and waits and waits, only to realize one fine day, that an entire lifetime has slipped by and her dreams have turned to dust.

The egg had cooked to a deep golden brown by the time Myra heard the shower go off. A couple of minutes later, Kairav walked into the kitchen followed by soap-scented steam, clean-shaven and barefoot, dressed in a ragged old pair of denim shorts and nothing else. He was still fit and lean, she noticed idly, his shoulders still solid, belly still flat and hard. And he could still make her heart give that silly little leap with just one lazy grin.

Ignoring the overpowering temptation to run her fingers down his belly and back, she simply smiled. "You look almost human again. Feel any better?"

"Actually, I feel like a hopeless fool," he mumbled. Walking across to her, he bent down to give her a peck on the cheek. "Sorry. I don't know what the hell I thought I was doing, grabbing you like that. I didn't mean anything by it."

As she knew all too well, Myra thought wearily. "Forget it, Kairav," she told him easily. "You're a man. And men do stupid things all the time. It's what makes you so appealing."

Refusing to think about it, she slid three thick slices of toast onto a plate along with some scrambled eggs and handed it to him.

"Eat this. You still look a little rough around the edges."

"I feel a little rough around the edges, too."

Grinning, he took the plate, and padded into the verandah, moving his fingers through his wet hair.

"I still can't believe I had the guts to tow you out of bed and all the way out here, just because I was feeling sorry for myself."

"You're allowed," she replied casually, carrying her own plate across to the table and sitting down.

"Most of the time you're an intelligent, competent businessman with a solid grip on his life and destiny. I figure you're entitled to one night of generalized stupidity, all considered. Just don't make it a habit."

Kairav winced slightly. "Point taken. Still friends?"

"Forever." She said it easily, the ritual as old as their friendship.

Kairav just nodded, eating the breakfast thoughtfully. He'd been thinking about Myra in the shower – a few sensational thoughts, granted, but it had been more than that. Thinking about how she was always there for him, about how he sometimes just took for granted that all he had to do was shout and she'd be there, calm and composed and in control.

"You, umm..." He looked at her thoughtfully. "You didn't really have someone with you when I called tonight, did you?"

Myra stared at him, fork halfway to her mouth. "What a question to ask!"

"You would tell me, wouldn't you? If you were getting serious about someone?"

"It's the strangest thing..." Myra cocked her head slightly, as though listening to something. "I could swear, I hear my mother. Didn't that just sound like my mother?"

"Alright, alright," he growled. "I know it's none of my business, but—"

"It *is* my mother!" She looked around with mock surprise, eyes as big as light bulbs. "I was sure she was in Delhi this week."

"Don't try and throw this change-the-topic tantrum on me, you wise princess," Kairav said with a straight face. "I'm dead serious, Myra." Realising, with some surprise, that he meant it. "We've never kept secrets from each other. I know you and that investment banker, Akhil or Nikhil or whatever his name is, have been seeing a lot of each other lately."

She leaned back with an exaggerated sigh, crossing her arms. "I presume you mean Akhil Arora, the investment banker you introduced me to last year. Yes, we have been seeing each other pretty often, or as often as possible, considering I live on one side of the country and he on the other. And no, he wasn't with me tonight. Nor was anyone else, for that matter. Happy?"

Kairav said, "So, you and he aren't...?" He lifted an eyebrow questioningly.

"Kairav!" She gave a burst of laughter. "It's none of your business if we are!" Still grinning, she looked at him with amusement. "Although, to prevent any more questioning, no, we are not...yet," she added mysteriously.

"Yet." Kairav's eyes narrowed slightly. "Meaning he's thinking about it."

"Of course, he's thinking about it. He's an eligible bachelor!"

"And you'd...?" He lifted his eyebrow again.

"Now that's really none of your business!"

"So you're thinking about it, too."

"Kairav!" Myra took a deep breath, and then let it out again with a quiet laugh. "I bet he would at least bring me flowers and wine before trying to peel me out of my jeans."

Kairav groaned. "I said I was sorry about that, damn it."

"Mmm." She looked at him for a moment, an odd expression on her face. "What I'm saying, Kairav, is that I just don't know how I feel about him. He's certainly everything a woman could want..."

Kairav gave a grunt, not liking the expression on her face. Not liking the idea of Akhil trying to peel her out of any damned thing, flowers or no flowers. "He's too old for you."

Myra's left eyebrow arched sluggishly. "Excuse me?"

"Well, hell, he's got to be forty if he's a day."

"Thirty-five."

"Like I said, he's too old for you."

"I like older men." There was a dangerous glow in her eyes.

"He's probably married."

"He's never been married."

"Never?" It was Kairav's turn to lift an eyebrow. "Don't you think that's strange? That this perfect eligible bachelor has never been married? Doesn't that tell you something about him?"

"It tells me," she said sweetly, "that he is considerably wiser than some men I could mention."

"Sounds to me as though he's got some sort of problem in the fun-and-games department or he is gay, I mean."

"Trust me," Myra shot back even more sweetly. "He has no problem in that area at all."

"I don't even want to know how you've figured that out if you haven't even—"

"Didn't you tell me just last week in that car showroom that you don't have to take a car out of the showroom to know whether it's going to be a great drive? Gut instinct, I think you said."

"I also mentioned experience," Kairav said slyly. "And I think I've had a bit more experience with cars than you've had with—"

"Do you have any idea at all of how thin that ice is, where you're standing?"

Kairav grinned, cutting into the toast with his fork. "Hey, I was just trying to make a point. If you like the guy, fine … go with what feels good. Just don't start getting serious about him or anything though, because—"

"He's asked me to marry him."

She said it quietly, without laughter or even a sly smile to soften it. Kairav nearly choked on a mouthful of toast. "He's what?" His yell made her blink.

"Marry you? He can't marry you! It's out of the damned question."

"And just why is it out of the question?"

"Because…" He didn't know for certain, Kairav realized, but there was no damned way he was going to let Myra, his Myra, marry some no-good financier and—

"Your business, for one thing," he said with satisfaction. "He lives in Mumbai. Your business is here. Commutation is impossible."

"Akhil lives in Bangalore," she said calmly. "His ancestral home is there, all twenty rooms of it. His head office is in Mumbai, but he's only there a couple of days a week."

"Even worse," Kairav growled. Bangalore is even farther away."

"Once we get the investment, I would quit the business, obviously."

"Over my dead body."

"That can be easily arranged, Kairav."

"You're my best friend. You can't move to Bangalore. What would I do without you?"

Something flickered across her face, gone before he could figure out what it was. "You'll manage, Kairav. You always do."

"That's not the point." He felt unsettled and angry for no real reason, and he frowned at her, reaching out suddenly to run his fingers down the silken sweep of her hair. "You're not really going to marry him, are you, Myra?"

"I don't know what you'd have to say about it if I did." She sounded impatient and a little angry herself, and there was a hint of colour across her cheeks. "I have a life of my own, Kairav. You seem to forget that sometimes. I have a right to be happy. My entire existence doesn't revolve around you, you know! Round and round and round." Kairav was following her index finger going round and round in the air between them, heavy with confusion and charged with strange sparks.

Kairav looked across the table at her, trying to read her expression. "Are you saying you're not happy?"

He mulled the thought over, trying to make some sense of it. "Are you saying—?"

"I'm not saying anything," she snapped, attacking a piece of toast and egg with her fork. "It's just that sometimes, I think you don't see me as a person at all. I'm just good old Myra, best friend material. I am there whenever you need me, the very dependable and solid friend. I am there for our business; I manage the bankers, the loan discussions and their payments, blah, blah, blah. I make sure our financial reporting is perfect for our investors. Not only that, I manage your personal life as well – your lunch, sometimes movies, your sad days, your health."

She put the fork down with a bang and looked up at him angrily. "My god, I don't know why you even bother about either of us getting married. I am doing everything that a good business partner and a wife would do, that is double benefit for you!"

Kairav simply stared at her, trying to figure out just what the hell he should be saying. Knowing fully well that whatever it would be, it had better be convincing. He hadn't seen her like this in a long time, had no idea what had set her off.

"Look, Myra," he said carefully, feeling his way cautiously through a verbal minefield, "I know I can be—"

"Forget it." She shoved her chair back and stood up, cheeks blushing slightly. "I know what you're going to say, and you're right. You can be a selfish, arrogant bastard at times. But this isn't about you, it's about me. I—"

She stopped abruptly, then just shrugged and managed a rough smile. "Oh, don't look so alarmed, Kairav. I'm not going to run off to Bangalore and marry Akhil or quit our business or throw dishes or anything. I'm just tired and I needed to let off some steam. Finish your breakfast while I take a shower, and I promise that by the time I come out, I'll be back to normal."

"Hey, Myra?" Kairav got to his feet in one easy move, reaching out to grab her arm gently as she turned to leave. "Hey, darling, I'm sorry. I had no right dragging you out of bed to come over here and hold my hand. And I sure as hell have no right trying to tell you who you should or shouldn't date or marry or sleep with or whatever. If you want go ahead with old Nikhil, hey, you've got my blessings."

For a split second, Myra was seriously tempted to plant her open palm across his cheek with every bit of strength she possessed, just to see if that would shake him up a bit. But even as the urge hit her, it vanished again, leaving her struggling not to laugh with the sheer impossibility of the man. "It's Akhil, for the last time. And no wonder women fall all over themselves to marry you, Kairav," she finally said. "You're the most romantic devil I've met in years!"

She put a fake smile on her lips and left him standing there with a puzzled expression on his handsome face, suddenly afraid that if she stayed in the room with him for even another instant, she'd give away her true feelings.

Four hours, three cups of coffee and a crisis or two later, Myra was still having trouble concentrating.

The memory of Kairav's strong, muscled body pressed intimately against hers, was just a little too vivid for comfort.

She'd be fine for a while, when her mind was focused on work with its usual laser-like intensity; but then, she'd remember the warmth of his breath on her throat or the way his toughened palm had moved across her body. Without warning, her breath would catch and her thoughts would go leaping off into all sorts of inappropriate directions; and she'd find herself sitting at her desk, staring blankly at some piece of paper, or looking up and seeing someone pinning her down with their hopeful gaze and realize that they'd asked her a question she had never even heard.

"If I didn't know better," her colleague finally said with an all-too-shrewd look, "I'd say you'd spent the night in the sack with some seriously hot guy, drinking champagne and making love until the sun came up."

"Champagne gives me the hiccups," Myra replied with a laugh, tossing down a handful of papers, "...and I never make love until sun-up the night before I have to put finishing touches on a buy-out offer worth crores." She grinned. "Seriously hot, huh? From that, am I given to understand that your daughter is home from college for spring break?"

Shruti Dewan grinned back. "Like, for real, babes. It's been three days now, and I haven't understood a word she's said. It's frightening when you think about it. I'm spending several thousand rupees to send a perfectly normal, well-spoken girl to the best college in Mumbai, and she comes back speaking in this crazy *Mumbaiya* language, with no visible literary line and completely under the thrall of a roomie whose main interests seem to be food and fashion."

"Oh, to be young and to be able to enjoy it is fun, Shruti. Let her enjoy it. When I was eighteen, I thought the world would stay a magic place forever. Now I'm almost thirty, and the only magic I seem to be able to summon up is time-shifting old movies on Netflix."

"That Akhil of yours looks like he should be able to summon up a thing or two," Shruti said slyly.

Myra nodded absently, leafing through a thick computer printout. "Has Finance sent down their revised estimates on this Info Capital deal yet? Kairav and I are going head-to-head with their CEO Kapil Kapoor and his Head of Finance on Friday. We need to add the figures to the project report."

Shruti reached across Myra's desk without saying a word, and tapped in a couple of commands on the computer. It flashed a working message for a moment or two, then spilled a multicoloured display of figures across the screen.

Myra gazed at it in silence, then glanced up at Shruti with a tiny smile. "I knew that."

Shruti just nodded, a tiny smile playing around her mouth. "Come over to dinner some night this week, okay? You and Ayesha can swap stories about college life. She thinks I'm too old to remember back that far."

Myra gave a sputter of laughter. Shruti was all of thirty-eight. "Sounds good. Pick an evening and tell me when."

"Thursday. Right after work."

"I thought you were going to the movies on Thursday night with that new guy in Product Design."

"Abhishek?" Shruti made a face. "We went out twice. The first time, he took me to a romantic restaurant; he spent the entire evening telling me all about his ex-wife. The second time, we went to an automobiles exhibition; he spent the entire day telling me all about his favourite cars. The third time he called, I told him I was down with chicken pox. He hasn't called again."

Myra groaned, laughing. "Oh, Shruti, I'm sorry! I sometimes think all the unattached men in this city come in two flavours – bizarre and seriously bizarre."

Shruti smiled dryly. "You got that right." The smile faded. "And the ones who aren't, just don't seem to be able to see what's right in front of them."

She could have been talking about Kairav, Myra thought, but she wasn't. Only Sachin could put that look of gloom on Shruti's usually cheerful face. "You could ask him over to dinner," she said gently. "Or to a movie."

"I know," Shruti said with a sigh. "If only he wasn't so shy! I think he's interested, Myra, I really do. But he doesn't seem to know what to do about it. Until I met him, I didn't know what a computer nerd was! It's all he seems to care about."

"Back when Kairav and I were in college, most of his friends were just like Sachin," Myra said sympathetically. "If a girl even looked at them, they'd stumble and drop things. Most of them started their own entrepreneurial ventures and are bazillionaires by now, but they still have social skills that sum up to a zero. It goes with the territory."

"Except for Kairav."

"Except for Kairav." Myra smiled. "He always did have more going for him than a triple-digit 10. He went from college, directly to the cool entrepreneur and bypassed the nerd stage altogether."

They stayed silent for a few moments, thinking of Kairav. Shruti had a soft spot for him too. Kairav hailed from a rich business family and his father was a jet-setter, his mum, a socialite. His family was the classic "it's all about money, honey"; and Kairav, it seemed, took his genes seriously. Entrepreneurship was in his blood.

Shruti looked like she wanted to say something. Then she just smiled. "Thursday evening, then. Chinese?"

"Love it."

"Good. I'll stock up on Chilli Chicken and Hakka Noodles and make it a night to remember. Ayesha's friend Akshita will be there, but she's an easy conversationalist. One groan means "no", two means "yes" and a shrug means she doesn't know."

"She doesn't talk?"

"Who knows? I've never seen her with her mouth empty long enough to find out."

"I can hardly wait to meet her. She sounds like some of the girls in my hostel who ate everybody's food, snatched the remote and saw TV programs of their choice in the common room."

Laughing, Myra pushed back her chair and got to her feet, grabbing up a handful of reports from the corner of her desk. "I have to go over these with Kairav. Hold my calls, unless it's someone from Info Capital."

"Did, um…?" Shruti winced. "Is Kairav… uhm… single again? I kinda overheard the two fighting on top of their voices when I went to his house to drop the financial documents. I suppose that means that the Navya female will have her claws in him soon."

Shruti's eyes glittered.

"For months now, she's been hovering around like a vulture waiting for an accident to happen. You can practically hear her salivating at the prospect of carrying in the catch of the day."

Shruti's metaphors may have been mixed, but they made their point.

"If she's serious about landing him, she's going to have to make a heavy-duty attempt," Myra said quietly. "One sign she's getting serious and he'll head for open water. He is allergic to commitment."

"Let's hope you're right." Picking up a handful of letters she had been going over and needed to mark for Kairav's attention, Shruti turned and headed back to her own office.

Myra stared blindly after her for a moment or two, then gave herself a mental shake and walked across to the door leading to Kairav's office. Navya Mehta. Interesting thought.

Shrewd, beautiful and as cold as ice, she headed a successful corporate law office in Delhi. An expert in corporate law and protecting intellectual property rights, her firm had guarded many entrepreneur start-ups from investment vultures by carefully studying all contracts and protecting them. She had wooed Kairav for almost a year before he'd shifted his firm UrbanFork over to her, and she'd never bothered to hide the fact that Kairav's business wasn't all she was interested in. So far, Kairav had held her at bay. But now…?

Myra was still frowning when she knocked on Kairav's door, pushing it open and entering.

Kairav's office ran the full width of the building, a peaceful retreat filled with modern art, with plenty of white furniture and gleaming glass windows letting in fresh sunlight. Her doing, of course. Had it been left to Kairav, he'd have nothing in here but a dozen custom-wired computers, a phone and a stack of discarded pizza and pasta boxes.

She smiled. Within the expensive suits and thousand rupee haircuts still lurked that frighteningly bright college kid whose passion for computer programming had given birth to a successful entrepreneurial venture which was now valued in crores.

"Hey, darling," he croaked, looking up as she came in.

"You look in fine shape," Myra replied calmly. "Head hurts, does it?"

Kairav managed a groan, then wished he hadn't. He closed his eyes gently and cautiously rubbed both temples. "I didn't think twelve-year-old Scotch gave you a hangover."

She disappeared behind him and poured something into a glass. "Consumed in reasonable quantities, I don't think it does."

"Cheap shot."

"Easy, anyway." She set something on the desk. "Drink up."

Kairav opened one eye and gazed blearily at the glass of bubbling liquid in front of him. "Quick or slow?"

"Quick. It tastes like hell."

"Is it going to kill me or cure me?"

"Do you really care?"

"No." Sitting back in his leather chair with another groan, Kairav reached for the glass and downed the contents in one long swallow, giving a shudder as it hit bottom. "You're enjoying this, aren't you?"

"Just a little." Smiling, she strolled around behind him and settled her hands on his shoulders, kneading them gently. "Take a couple of deep breaths and repeat after me. I will never drink half a bottle of Scotch at one go."

"Don't mention Scotch," Kairav groaned. "Don't mention stomach."

"I set up a meeting with Programming at twelve. I called Sachin Jain and asked him to bring his whole team with him."

Kairav nodded his head and then relaxed against the warmth of her hands working on his shoulders in a meticulous and affectionate way.

"So we're still having quality-control problems with the app. The app continues to malfunction, and transactions are not being completed. Sachin swears the problem isn't with the API integration, but with something in the programming code."

"And Programming swears the problem's in the UI integration."

Kairav flexed his shoulders, wincing slightly as a jolt of pain shot through his skull.

"That interface is sound, Myra. I went over the workflow with Sachin five dozen times. The damn thing should work."

"So there's a bug in the programming then," Myra said thoughtfully.

"Seems so. Wherever the hell it is, though, we've got to track it down fast. We need to launch the revised version asap to show our investors that UrbanFork is innovative and ahead of the competition. Hell, we have already informed them we are almost ready with the upgrade."

UrbanFork, the first app that Kairav and Myra had launched, now drew nearly five million users to it every month. A food delivery and dining out app, UrbanFork guided people to good restaurants, read reviews about it, check menus, book a table, or order food to be delivered home.

The app considered every aspect of food that a customer could think of. Just suppose you wanted "Chopsuey". All you had to do was put it in search and it would list every restaurant in the vicinity that offered it on their menu, by their rankings. It allowed you to search by cuisine, neighbourhood, and ranking, even offering chats with chef and customized dinners. The app also captured customer preferences, refining their choices, displaying more.

Kairav groaned again, this time in frustration. He tipped his head forward so she could massage the nape of his neck. "What's your take on the situation?"

"Our programming team is the best in the business. There is something we are missing, Kairav. Something obvious that we are not seeing."

"Such as?"

"I don't know." The rhythmic motion of her fingers paused as she thought about it, then resumed their slow massage of his neck muscles. "I am wondering if the problem could be with AllPay... The transaction hangs at precisely the moment you click that button..."

"The payment gateway!" Forgetting his aching head, Kairav sat straight up. "So the integration..."

"Yes, Kairav. It could be the integration of the payment gateways. Maybe the payment gateways which connect our app to all the credit/debit/mobile wallets have an issue. Maybe the gateway is picking only one instance/one restaurant order, and not multiple."

Kairav was already reaching for the phone. "I'm going down to the Programming floor to talk with Bhavik. You call AllPay and tell them I need to have their integration team here, now!"

"On it," Myra said, already heading for the door. "Let's see if this is the fix that has been eluding us."

Grinning, Kairav watched Myra as she strode out of the room, his hangover unbelievably gone. "Tell that Akhil of yours that if he wants to marry you, he'll have to go through me to do it," he called after her.

You're mine!

Hell, he'd not be able to move up without her, he thought as he waited for someone down in Programming to pick up the phone. It sent a chill down his spine, just the thought of losing her. But still he wouldn't commit, because he was afraid of commitments.

There was no one else in the company whose judgement he trusted as much as he trusted hers. She didn't just know the business inside out, she knew him just as intimately. She was able to finish his thoughts for him while he was still struggling to put an idea into words, was able to follow his leaps of logic when he was sorting through a problem, while everyone else stood around trying to figure out what he was talking about.

She was his sounding board when he needed to talk an idea through, and had enough solid ideas of her own that he'd learned to listen to. She could cut through the clutter to the heart of a problem faster than anyone else he knew too, playing the devil's advocate when she needed to, knowing which questions to ask, which issues to raise.

Besides, unlike most people who worked for him, she wasn't afraid of him. She tolerated his sporadic lapses in temper, ignored his bellows of impatience, told him to shut up now and again when she got tired of listening to him rage and talk wildly over some problem.

He grinned. Everyone else just ran for cover and lay low until the storm blew over. But Myra always seemed to take things, and him, in her stride. She was rarely rattled, never confused, his small spot of calm in an otherwise wise chaotic world.

He thought back to his encounter with her this morning. Of how she'd felt in his arms, all feminine softness and warmth, of the taste of her skin, her hair, her mouth. It had surprised him a little, how right she'd felt there. And her strong response had surprised him just as much; he hadn't realized until then just how damned sexy she was, how much he'd enjoy making love to her again. How much he had enjoyed it twelve years ago, he reminded himself with an inward smile. Strange, how a man could forget something like that until it all came rushing back, every detail of it, of her, so clear, it could have been merely a night ago.

He realized what he was doing suddenly and sat upright with a quick oath, irritated at his own wandering thoughts. He had to stop this. She'd kill him if she even suspected he was thinking of that night of those many years ago, let alone remembering it in fond detail.

And this morning... This morning had nearly been the mistake of his life.

It had been too easy, reaching for her like that. Too comfortable. Granted, it had been a hell of a long dry spell since Tanya had walked out, but a little sexual deprivation hadn't killed a man yet. Simple lust was no excuse to ruin the best friendship he'd ever had, or would ever have. So unless he was prepared to lose Myra completely, he had to make damned sure that he kept things strictly business between them from now on.

Myra glanced at her watch, frowning at how quickly the morning was slipping by. Bhavik and Sachin would be in the third-floor meeting room in another half hour. And if she wasn't there to referee, they'd be at each other's throats in minutes, each convinced that the other was responsible for the issues the app was facing.

It wasn't that neither wanted to take responsibility; it was just that both felt more loyalty to Kairav's UrbanFork, and Kairav, than they did to each other. They wanted the UrbanFork app to work. And took it very personally when it didn't.

Her phone gave a subdued chime and she reached for it absently, doing some quick mental calculations on the figures for the refreshed version of the app. On schedule and under budget, so far. She made a mental note to congratulate Bhavik.

The desk phone rang.

"Myra," Shruti said into her ear, "Trouble's on its way."

"Trouble?" Instinctively, Myra looked up at her office door. "Who and what?"

"Killer shark," Shruti said with a chuckle. "Good luck."

"Killer what?"

But Shruti had put the receiver down with a click, and before Myra could figure out what on earth she was talking about, her office door swung open and a swirl of white silk, a swinging shimmering swathe of glossy hair and expensive perfume came through.

Myra felt her hackles rise. "Good morning, Navya. It's nice to see you."

"I doubt that," Navya Mehta said, with a quiet laugh. She smiled down at Myra. "Protective little enclave you have here, isn't it? I have to practically submit to a strip search to get a visitor's badge from security, then I have to fight my way by Shruti to get in here."

Smiling with equal warmth – that is to say, none at all – Myra leaned well back in her chair, legs crossed, and eyed the intruder calmly. "You could go right in, but he's not there."

"In a meeting, I suppose." Navya's eyes drifted towards the connecting door to Kairav's office, as though suspecting a lie.

"No, he's down on the Programming floor somewhere."

"And I suppose calling him on his mobile phone is out of the question?"

"I wouldn't suggest it. He doesn't like being interrupted when he's busy."

"Not even for me?" The smile was bold. The eyes were bolder.

"Not even for me." Check and mate.

"Mmm. Serious indeed." Navya's smile was as cool as the pale blue lenses in her eyes.

As always, she was dressed for battle, clad in white silk trousers and a coordinated pink tube top, over which she'd carelessly tossed a brilliant white Promod jacket. The effect was dazzling and expensive, and had probably created whiplash up and down the street as she had walked to the office building.

"So, our mutual friend is single again, I hear."

"I am not here to discuss Kairav's personal life, Navya," Myra said with a smile. "You should know that by now."

"True. Getting information out of you is like prying money out of one of my ex-boyfriends." Shoving her hands in her jacket pockets, she gazed down at Myra companionably. "I suppose it's only courtesy to inform you that I have my eye on him."

Myra bit back a hostile reply and smiled gently. "Well, then I suppose it's only fair to tell you that you're just one of the many, Navya."

She was amused to see a flash of annoyance deep in the other woman's eyes.

She let her smile widen. "I figure that by the time word gets around, he'll be knee-deep in women with designs comparable to yours."

Navya didn't smile back.

"And what about you, Myra? I get the impression you may be interested in him yourself."

"Dating your business partner isn't good for business, Navya."

"Oh, I don't know. It's been a long while since I worked with anyone but myself, but I seem to remember that dating someone forbidden added a bit of excitement to the day. Although I suggest that if you decide to indulge in some mid-day desktop lovemaking, lock the office door unless you want to startle the secretarial staff."

Myra had to laugh.

"Have you taken a good look at the top of Kairav's desk lately? Making love on it would be like making love in a gadget showroom. His desktop is littered with gizmos!"

To her surprise, Navya gave a snort of genuine laughter. "God, he's like a kid with all that electronic junk, isn't he? We were in his car last week, we stopped at a red light, and the next thing I know he's got his window down and is talking with a couple sitting on a bike asking them how they choose a restaurant on a weekend. He handed them two-three mobile phones and began asking on which one they felt the app was working better. Can you believe that?"

"If you're serious about him, you'd better get used to it. And it would be a good idea if you learned how to test his app on different mobile phones, too."

Navya shuddered delicately. "I don't think so, thanks." She displayed long-tapered fingernails painted the exact shade of pink and white as her tube and jacket. "I'm certain I can interest Kairav in games of a more personal nature."

Myra's thoughts briefly wandered to being in Kairav's arms that morning; she could still almost feel the curved strength in his lean body as he'd pressed against her, wanting, needing her badly.

"I have no doubt of that," she said with forced calm, fighting the temptation to launch herself at Navya's slender throat. Killing Navya wouldn't do much good in the long run. Another woman would simply take her place.

Trying to keep women away from Kairav was like trying to keep bees away from honey.

"Well..." Navya made an exaggerated show of looking at her watch. "I can't spend all morning here. Are you sure you can't call Kairav and tell him I'm here?"

"I have no idea when he will be back," Myra said quite truthfully. "And he will not answer his mobile. It could take twenty minutes to track him down, and even then, there's no guarantee he'll stop whatever he's doing to respond. He could be down there all afternoon."

Navya's expression darkened and she glared at the door to his office helplessly. "Tell him I was here, will you?"

"Of course. Does he have your number?"

Low hit below the belt. It earned her a cool look.

"You know he does, Myra. And trust me, honey, I have yours."

Counter-hit.

Myra had her mouth open to make a pointed retort when the door banged open and Kairav walked in, grinning broadly. His expensively-tailored suit jacket was tossed carelessly over one broad shoulder, the top two buttons of his Hugo Boss shirt undone, Tie Rack's tie hanging loose around his neck. His hair was tousled as though he'd run his fingers through it in frustration and he was flaunting a wide grin.

"You were right, darling! Have I told you lately that I love you?"

Navya Mehta was leaning against the corner of Myra's desk, looking like a crisp two thousand rupee note, as usual.

She turned towards him with an expectant smile, as Kairav walked across the room. He gave her a nod of acknowledgement as he stepped past her and leaned down to give a satisfying kiss squarely on Myra's cheek.

Trying to ignore a distinctive and erotic stirring low in his belly, he grinned and sat beside her chair, feeling like a five-year-old kid who had aced a difficult math problem. "You got it in one hit. It was a sixer on the first ball. I owe you big for this one...you probably saved this deal."

She grinned back, eyes twinkling. "So... it was the integration! That was the issue."

"Yes, our mobile wallet partner AllPay have discovered a coding error in their program that stops the two APIs from synching in. Now they are gonna fix it!"

He leaned across to give her another quick peck. "You've earned yourself a raise in your stock options, girl."

Myra laughed, looking as genuinely pleased at having the problem solved as he was. "So I can cancel the meeting with Bhavik and Sachin?"

"Already took care of it. They are best buddies again. Crisis avoided, thanks to you, my dear."

He smiled. "Don't know what I'd do without you." Another quick kiss and he was on his feet, looking around to smile at Navya this time. "Hello, Navya darling. Here to take me to lunch?"

"Forget it," Myra shot back, her eyes glittering slightly. "We have to go over these figures again before this afternoon's meeting. Make it dinner, or reschedule."

Navya smiled, reaching up to caress his cheek, her fingers remaining there for a moment.

"She takes such good care of you, doesn't she?" she said sweetly.

There was something in her voice, in the very air around them, that made Kairav look first at her, then at Myra. Both smiled, as charming as cats about to start a ring fight over a mouse!

And as deadly, Kairav thought uneasily. There was something a little dangerous in Myra's eyes, and Navya's pink fingernails flashed slightly as she removed her hand from his cheek.

Now what? He knew Myra didn't like Navya much, but there seemed to be an extra indication of hostility in the air today, a sense of something going on that he couldn't quite put a finger on.

Not that he deluded himself into thinking that he'd figure it out in this lifetime. The complexities and rituals of female politics had always puzzled the hell out of him. Actually he never wanted to understand them. He'd decided a long time ago that the smartest thing a man could do was keep his head down and his butt safely out of the line of fire.

"Come on in and I'll pour you a cup of coffee," he said easily, putting his hand on Navya's back and guiding her gently, but firmly towards his office.

As the door closed behind them, he walked across to the glass table near the wall of windows overlooking Delhi's busy roads. He took the coffee jug and poured two cups of the special blend he had at office. He handed one to Navya. "Cheers."

"More aptly, congratulations."

"For?"

Navya's mouth curved up in a gentle smile. "For finally getting rid of serious girlfriend number two. It must feel *nice*, not having *that* hanging over you anymore. I always used to call you Mr. No-Commitment, and you always live up to it."

"Nice isn't the word I would have chosen," Kairav said quietly. He still hadn't entirely gotten used to the idea of being single, even if it was just in bed. He thought ofTanya now, deliberately testing his memory for pain; and bumped into nothing but worn-out sadness. Maybe he *was* Mr. No-Commitment, Mr. No-feelings-for-Ex and Mr. I-don't-care or whatever!

"How did you find out? Don't tell me it's out in the newspapers," he said sarcastically.

"A friend told a friend who told a friend, and she told a friend who called me last evening. I was going to drop by, but I had a dinner meeting that ran till a bit late into the night."

Kairav thought of the half-empty bottle of Scotch sitting on his bar at home.

"Probably good you didn't. I would have made awful company."

"Oh, I'm sure I could have come up with an idea or two guaranteed to raise your spirits. And who knows what else..." She spoke in a tone that bordered on seduction and molestation. "Come on, Kairav, lighten up! You look like *Devdas*, sitting in despair and mooning over nothing important."

He managed a rough smile. "It's probably just the hangover."

"Ahh." She gave a smile. "I see. It was that way, was it?"

He grunted something vaguely affirmative and walked across the room to drop into one of the big armchairs by the window.

He usually enjoyed conversations involving smart comebacks with Navya, but he was tired today. The kind of tired that went deep inside and made him feel as if he'd never get free of it.

"So, what can I do for you Navya?"

"God, so formal." She kicked off her high heels and padded across to drop gracefully into the chair across from his. Lifting one long, rounded leg, she settled her bare foot on his lap. "You know why I'm here, Kairav. I put a proposition to you a month ago. I'm still waiting for your answer."

Kairav settled both hands around her small foot and started massaging it. "I didn't think you were serious, Navya."

"Dead serious." She arched her foot, sighing in pleasure as he massaged her. "I want you to live with me. No strings, no fancy expectations, just satisfying our mutual interests. We could just live and sleep together and save the lawyers' fees. You know I do not believe in marriages and so do you." She laughed. "Hell, I've been trying to get you into my bed for long, Kairav, but have had no success so far."

"I was in a relationship with Tanya, for god's sake."

"You were separated at heart. You and Tanya hadn't much left, for the last few months. It was pretty evident to everyone."

"A relationship is a relationship, no matter what's evident to everyone and what not," he said quietly. "It's like being pregnant, Navya – no halfways or almosts. I may not be able to make my relationships work, but I damned well won't sleep around while I am in one."

She gave a small sigh of what might have been frustration. "As you made abundantly clear the last time I flung myself at you, dear man. But the point is arguable now. You are no longer in a relationship. That means you can do what the bunnies do, repeatedly and with enthusiasm. In fact, if I had the time, we could do it right here, right now."

Kairav looked up at her uneasily, not knowing if she was just teasing or had something else on her mind. You never quite knew with Navya. But to his relief, she didn't seem inclined to start flinging her clothes off, and he relaxed again. "I've just broken up! Why in god's name would I be interested in getting into another relationship again?"

"Because I'm not Tanya. Or Ria. I don't pretend to be in love with you, nor am I deluding myself into thinking you're in love with me. We're both wounded, both wary, both tired of the rubbish that comes with the relationship certificate. I've had two great affairs in eight years, and each one told me he loved me and then, six months after the start, started trying to change me into the person he thought I should be."

She drew her foot from his grasp and tucked it under her, leaning forward slightly. "Kairav, I'm thirty years old and I am one successful corporate lawyer. I'm a workaholic; I don't have the inclination, or the disposition to be the sweet corporate wife. Most of the eligible men I know cannot handle my success, my temperament or my hours."

"And you think I can?" He was intrigued in spite of himself.

"I know you can. You're as obsessed about your work as I am about mine, so the fact that I spend most of my time in the office wouldn't bother you. And you're man enough not to be bothered about my success and money."

She smiled. "You know as well as I do how cold it is out here in the big world of corporate success, Kairav. I'd like to come home at night and have someone there, someone warm and uncomplicated. When I have a business or charity function to attend, I'd like to go with a man I respect and admire, not the stud-of-the-week. I'm tired of playing the field. I like you. We seem to fit together pretty well. And I think it makes sense."

"So it's sort of the ultimate joint venture!"

"That's one way of looking at it."

"Pretty cold."

"You have tried to be in a steady relationship twice, Kairav," she said quite brutally. "Look where it got you."

There was no denying that she had a point. Not with the ink still wet on his second break-up.

After a long pause he said, "Is this a one-shot opportunity, or can I think about it for a few days?"

She laughed out loud. "I hardly expect you to jump into another relationship just after your last one ended, Kairav. But think about it. Take as long as you need, but don't take forever." Smiling, she slid to her feet and eased herself across his lap, with a leg on either side of his.

"Of course, I could give you an added incentive right now... if you've got a few minutes." Her hand glided playfully downward.

Kairav caught her wrist firmly. "I thought you were in a hurry."

"I am. But I can be really fast and really good."

"A talent I've never mastered," he said calmly, turning his head to avoid her kiss. "I have a meeting in about ten minutes, sweetheart, so don't get your engine started."

"You're too young to be a stuffy old man, Kairav. Ten minutes is plenty of time to satisfy both parties involved if you get right down to business." She moved her legs suggestively.

"It takes me longer than ten minutes just to figure out which shirt to wear in the morning," Kairav said with a laugh. "Cool down, Navya." Even if he weren't hung over, her offer held all the appeal of a hit-it-enjoy-it-forget-it-incident.

To his relief, she laughed good-naturedly, kissed his cheek lightly, then swung off his lap and straightened her jacket.

"We would be good together, Kairav. You know it and I know it. So think over what I said and get back to me."

She looked at her watch and frowned. "Damn, I'm late! I have a major meeting in less than an hour with the top shots of a big investment firm. If I can convince them we can save them a few crores in tax write-offs a year, their business will be worth a fortune. Wish me luck."

"You've got it." He got to his feet, suddenly distracted. Investments made him think of Akhil Arora, which made him think of Myra, which made him think of her threat to marry and move to Bangalore and have babies and walk on Brigade Road and MG Road hand in hand or whatever the hell they did up there, leaving him and UrbanFork to fend for themselves. "And I'll, uh, call."

"Damn right you will, Kairav. Or I'll have your head on a non-veg platter." A quick peck on the cheek, and she was gone.

The door had barely closed behind her when it opened again and Kairav glanced up, half expecting her to come flying back in to finish what she'd tried to start. But it was Myra, looking as cool and serene as always, although there was a glitter in her eyes that boded no good for anyone who got in her way.

"She says you're going to get involved with her."

Kairav rubbed his forehead, squeezing his eyes closed for a moment. "The topic came up, yeah. But don't run out and buy us a gift quite yet, darling. It ain't over 'til it's over."

"I've bought you many anniversary gifts in the past twelve years," she said with an edge to her voice. "You don't get another."

Kairav leaned well back in the soft armchair and looked at her. "Relax, Myra. I'm not getting into another relationship or marriage right now." Though he had started thinking about it already. After all, he was actually an "I-break-up-and-hit-back-soon" kind of person.

"Although, to quote a good friend of mine from just this morning, 'I don't know what you'd have to say about it if I did'."

Her head lifted and she levelled a look at him that he'd seen bring strong men to their knees.

"I think, as someone told me just this morning, that I have some right to know if you're going to get involved or marry that woman—" she bit the words out like poison "—for no other reason than twenty years of friendship."

Kairav opened his mouth to deny it, then sighed, rubbing his forehead, wishing his head would stop pounding.

"Hell, Myra, I've had worse offers. I got into a relationship with Ria because I thought I loved her, and I went in for Tanya thinking I was in love with her. And right now, I'm sitting here thinking maybe, just maybe, that it's not the 'staying together' part that gets me into trouble, but the 'being in love' part. Maybe there is no such thing. Maybe the girl I love doesn't exist. Maybe I should just live with someone I don't hate too much, and take it from there."

Something crossed her face, maybe a shadow, a hint of pain, gone in an instant. He looked at her curiously, expecting her to say something, but she just turned away and walked to the door. And as he watched the door close behind her, the thought hit him that if he had any sense at all, he'd talk her into marrying him right now. But he wouldn't, because he was Mr. No...yes, hell, that!

Although, he reminded himself as an afterthought, he couldn't marry his best friend. Because then she wouldn't be his best friend anymore, she'd be his wife. And then who would he turn to when the break-up came through?

▼

Myra was still sitting mad a couple of hours later.

Damn it, no one, absolutely no one, could be crazy enough to jump into one relationship while barely disentangled from the last one. And Kairav, Kairav was about the least crazy person she'd ever met. Except when it came to women, she amended, fighting a surge of renewed fury. Heaven knows, she'd decided not long after he'd lived with Tanya, that it was a defective gene he had or something. Some sort of chemical imbalance that could turn a highly intelligent entrepreneur into a complete idiot almost overnight.

Granted, he hadn't had a fighting chance with Tanya. She had finalized him on the basis of perfect parameters that could be fitted in a 'perfect partner' matrix. Kairav had been everything Tanya had wanted in a husband. He was a self-made man, poised to hit the big time, well-mannered and handsome. He didn't slurp his coffee or fumble with his cutlery; he wore a Tie Rack tie like some fashion armour and could charm anyone in his company. He could choose a good wine, a good restaurant, drive a fast car and handle a fast woman just as well. On top of that, he knew people. Important people. And to a young and very ambitious businesswoman, that was irresistible.

For her part, Tanya was probably what Kairav *thought* he wanted in a life partner. Gorgeous. Intelligent. Highly successful. They'd made a spectacular couple for the first year or so, but then, little by little, the dream had started to tarnish.

Less than two years after he and Tanya had been together, Kairav had become withdrawn, reserved and sullen-eyed, snapping at anyone who came too near, working crazy hours and travelling needlessly, shutting himself off. Myra had stayed out of it until New Year's Eve of that third year, when he'd turned up on her, telling her date to get the hell out, and he'd poured himself a triple shot of whisky, downing it in one long swallow; then he'd flung the glass against the wall with a string of oaths that had made her stare at him in astonishment.

And then he'd told her about Tanya. About the fight they'd had. Tanya had only been with him to fastrack her career, and wanted nothing but that, and was not willing to relax a little with him and enjoy some of the perks of her success.

She was gone, he'd added tightly. She'd told him she was tired of it, tired of him. She was breaking up with him.

In the following weeks, Kairav's mood had gone from bad to worse. Then he'd shaken it off and had picked up the pieces of his life.

Except he'd been different afterward. More introspective. Quieter. Laughing less, spending more time alone. And a little colder, as though he'd shut off a part of himself and had no intention of ever letting anyone that close to him again.

Myra swore tiredly. If she had any sense, she'd go home. Order in a salad for dinner. Have a long soak in her bath tub, up to her neck in boiling hot water with aroma salts, creep into bed and just sleep until—

Her phone cried, supporting her mood, and she reached for it wearily. "Yes?"

"Mr. Kapoor and his COO Ratan Jogani are here, Myra."

"Here?" Myra sat straight up. "Now what!"

She shot to her feet, grabbing her jacket off the back of her chair, pulling it on as she hopped around on one foot, trying to get her heels back on. She popped her head into Kairav's office and told him, then, pausing long enough to run a comb through her hair and freshen her make-up, she took a deep breath and walked out into the reception area.

Ratan Jogani saw her first. Grinning, he walked across and took her hand, leaned forward and kissed her cheek in greeting. Embarrassed, Myra stepped back.

Ratan's grin, however, widened. "I nearly called you last night. A couple of *'Dear Liar'* tickets fell into my lap at the last minute, and I remembered you saying you like to watch theatre shows."

"Oh my god! This is the Indian adaptation of the Broadway play. And that too with great actors like Naseeruddin Shah and Ratna Pathak Shah in lead roles!" Myra said excitedly.

"Forget theatre." Kairav walked in just in time to catch Ratan's offer. As he strolled across to join them, he found himself eyeing Ratan speculatively. "Unless we can come to an agreement on this deal, you and I are not together in business. And I'll consider any move you try making on my people as hostile." He smiled pleasantly enough as he said it, but there was a hint of very real jealousy under the words, which he didn't realize.

Who the hell did this dog think he was, anyway, asking Myra for a date? Especially here, in Kairav's own territory?

Ratan just grinned, seemingly untroubled, his grip firm as he shook Kairav's hand. "All the more incentive to get this deal hammered out and the money in the bank, eh?" He glanced at Myra, the smile warm. "I've always been partial to theatre myself."

Kairav had the sudden irrational urge to suggest that if he liked the damn musical theatre so much, why didn't he go there and watch *'Dear Liar'* rather than hitting on Myra? But he hung on to his temper, reminding himself that the deal with Info Capital wasn't in the bag yet. And on top of that, he was already walking on thin ice as far as Myra was concerned.

So he simply smiled mildly instead. "Our meeting was set up for Friday. What's the problem?"

"That's one of the reasons I like you so damn much, Kairav," a voice said from behind them. "You remind me of me. Straight to the point, and no wasting time."

Kairav turned around just as Kapil Kapoor came through the wide glass doors from the outer corridor.

He was built like a small building, not too tall but as solid as concrete, with thick grey hair, deceivingly mild eyes and an organized smile.

Kairav just nodded, waiting for it. Kapil Kapoor was a thorough, deliberate man, a financial analyst in his own right, who knew just which horse to back. Kairav respected him more than anyone else in the industry.

Then, abruptly, the friendly smile vanished and those mild eyes hardened to cold steel."I've gone over the last proposal you presented, and I still have some questions about some of your implementation and processes, Kairav."

"Then let's talk."

"I'll be honest with you, Kairav. Some of our people think we should think a bit longer and see if there are other start-ups which show more promise than yours. Whether it makes any sense for us to put money on you and if you are here for the long haul."

"This is what I built, Kapil," Kairav said. "For me, at this point, UrbanFork has not even reached first base. I have so many dreams for it, I have a long way to go before I sleep…"

Kairav relaxed slightly, smiling. "But yes, like my proposal detailed, there will be some sharp organizational and operational changes made once the investment comes in, to make us more efficient and cost-effective."

Kapil gazed at Kairav for a long, searching moment, then nodded abruptly.

"Hmmm… I want to see your business plan and forecasted revenues once again," said Kapil, "Take me through them once more, so I perfectly understand where you are coming from after having read what you sent me."

Ratan added, "Some of our analysts are not convinced by your projections. I will also need to sit with Myra once to go through the capital requirements. I want to iron out the sticky parts, the projections may need some tweaking."

Kairav fought his impatience. He wanted this deal tied up now, not sometime next week or the week after or—

Myra caught his eye just then and gave an almost unnoticeable shake of her head in warning. Kairav let out a tight breath. The girl could read his mind like an astrologer. Knew him better than he knew himself sometimes. He mustered a grin and kept quiet.

"May I make a suggestion?" Ratan looked at Kairav thoughtfully. "It's just a matter of getting the numbers right. What you and Kapil need to do to finalize this deal, is to simply sit down and talk this through once today's agenda is done. Am I right?"

Kairav smiled. "I'm certainly willing."

Kapil reverted, "So am I."

Ratan fought a surge of satisfaction, keeping his expression blank, smart enough to work his magic in spending more time with Myra, while the deal was on.

"Then I suggest we all meet here, in your boardroom over the weekend. Let's take Saturday and Sunday to really thrash this out. We need to get more traction on your expansion plans and financial ratios, than it comes across on paper. There are also plenty of queries from the team. So if your team is available to share them across the table, things can be done faster. Can we do that?"

Kapil looked at Ratan in surprise. "That," he said after a thoughtful moment, "is a damned good idea. Kairav?"

Kairav nodded. He just wanted to get over with this. "Perfect. We've all been running in circles with this thing for weeks and everyone's tired. One last round of discussions, one on one, just might wrap it all up."

"Do it." Kapil looked at his watch. "I have to go. Set things up, talk with Ratan about anything you need. Just be on the ball with all the information we may need. I'll be there with my people."

"Sounds great." Ratan smiled down at Myra. "Maybe we'll get a chance to spend some time talking about something other than business while we're about it."

Myra's smile widened. "That would be—"

"Unlikely," Kairav cut the sentence midway, not liking the way Ratan was standing so damned close to her. Not liking the way he was still holding her hand after shaking it, either. Not liking anything at all about the man, as a matter of fact. Not his smile, the cut of his clothes, the way he carried himself – none of it.

"We've got a lot of details left to work out. I doubt we're going to have much time for socialising." Myra gave him a stern look, but Kairav ignored her.

"Come on Kapil, will take you through our business plan again," said Kairav, leading the way to his cabin. "We will then step out and you can have a word with our team heads if you wish."

Ratan, meanwhile, followed Myra to her cabin to go through the financials and the documentation. He had a huge check-list which he wanted clarifications on. Some of them, Myra could not clear right there and now. She would have to generate more reports, more figures… There was a lot to do. She made a check-list of all that needed to be done.

A couple of hours later, the duo from Info Capital was ready to go. The oncoming weekend was fixed for the meetings, and it was agreed that Saturday and Sunday, however long it took, it would be wrapped up. "Then the next week or so, our analysts can get to the final leg," said Kapil, "And we would be able to wrap up the deal soon."

And finally, after another round of handshaking and smiles – too damn much of each in Ratan's case, to Kairav's way of thinking – the two men left.

Kairav headed back through Myra's office to his own, unsettled and irritable for some reason, thinking about the way Myra had been looking at Ratan. Almost as though she actually liked the jerk, Kairav thought in annoyance. As though she couldn't see through the high-priced suit and expensive haircut to the smoothie corporate schmuck underneath.

"Well, that certainly was interesting." Myra followed him into his office, closing the door behind her and walking across to help herself to a cup of coffee.

"Yeah." Kairav dropped into his leather chair and leaned back, looking around at her. "That was a good idea you had out there, taking negotiations over the weekend."

"Firstly, I never gave that idea. It was Ratan. And secondly, I wasn't even talking about that, I was talking about the way you cut Ratan off at the knees out there." She strolled around to the front of his desk, a cup of steaming coffee in her hand. "You have a problem with him or something?"

"The kid's a jerk," Kairav muttered, reaching up to loosen his tie.

"Kid?" Myra's voice was filled with laughter. "He's the same age you are, Kairav."

"In years, maybe. But you know what they say, honey...it's not in the age, it's in the mileage."

"Mmm." She nodded, still watching him with that slightly thoughtful expression. "Competition making you a little jumpy?"

"Competition?" Kairav gave a snort. "I own this company. And him? He works for someone! Where's the competition?"

"That's not the kind of competition I was talking about. Although last week you told me how sharp he seemed to be."

"That was last week," Kairav smartly changed his statement.

"And then, there were his suggestions for the app. Last week you said that the ideas he had suggested would set the entire industry on its ear."

"Like I said, that was last week." Kairav pulled a stack of papers towards him, then shoved it away again.

"What's with you and this guy, anyway?" He gave her a sceptical look. "Funny. I never heard you say anything about liking theatre before," he said sarcastically.

"Why would I?" Myra's eyes flashed. "Your idea of a night out is lots of jarring music at the club and drinking all night."

"Since when did you get to be such a theatre lover? I've been with you to movies and you never mentioned that you like theatre more."

"I thought you liked movies, so..." she said indignantly.

"The question is, does Ratan like you?"

Myra stared at him for a full beat. "And just what is that supposed to mean?"

Kairav had his mouth half open to tell her exactly what it meant, then realized that he didn't know himself.

"Nothing," he muttered, running his fingers through his hair. "Hell, Myra, it didn't mean anything, alright? I'm just hung over and tired, and this whole Info Capital deal's got me wired tight. I thought we had everything going smooth as silk, and now I'm not so sure."

Myra eyed him mistrustfully for another moment or two, then finally nodded, relaxing. "It's going to be alright, Kairav. Kapoor just wants to get all the loose ends tied, that's all."

"Damn it, we are primed for growth and we have everything going for us, he knows that."

Myra had to smile, hearing the frustration in Kairav's voice.

"Relax. He's just getting prenuptial jitters. You have heard of his famed thoroughness. He needs to get to dot every 'i' and cross every 't', that's all."

"I said I'll take care of them, damn it," Kairav said angrily. "What the hell does he want from me, blood?"

"Your time. And as much as you can give in reports."

Kairav gave a thoughtful grunt. Then, almost grudgingly, he smiled, running his fingers through his already tousled hair again. "You're right, as always. Tell admin I want everything checked once in the meeting rooms, so that we have no glitches over the weekend. I will send them a mail before this hour is out, on a few other things. And yes, I want you to tell Sachin and Bhavik to be here. Maybe a few others you think may be crucial. And tell them all, no questions and no loose talk."

"I will do that. On your part Kairav, take a deep breath and get the AllPay issue fixed."

"Yes, I will." He flashed her a quick grin. "Hell, anyway, the weekend has no attraction for me. I'd rather spend it working."

"I'm sure Navya will be only too glad to take care of that for you," Myra said sweetly. Just the thought of Navya Mehta in bed with Kairav made her blood boil, but she smiled determinedly and pushed her chair back, getting to her feet. "I'll get my act in place."

"Hey!" Kairav reached out and caught her by the arm as she went to walk by him. Leaning back in his leather armchair, he let her arm slide through his grasp until he was holding her hand, fingers meshed with hers. "There's nothing between Navya Mehta and me, alright? Yeah, we've gone out a few times. And yeah, she made me an offer this morning that most men would give their right arm for. But I'm not interested."

Myra smiled carelessly, praying he couldn't read anything in her eyes. He knew her so damned well, it was hard to hide anything from him. Yet at times it was as though he didn't know her at all.

"I'm not your keeper, Kairav," she reminded him with a smile. "You don't have to tell me your plans."

"I know I don't," he said with a hint of impatience. "But this thing with Navya seems to be sticking in your head for some reason, and I just want to put your mind at ease. I'm not in love with her, I'm not going to marry her, I'm not going to marry anyone."

A grin flickered across his mouth. "I'd rather marry you. What do you say… we run off to Shimla for the weekend, get hitched and spend a few days in bed and—"

"You should be so lucky," she said with a reckless laugh, bending down to kiss him on the cheek just so he couldn't see her eyes.

Kairav turned his head at the last instant and to her surprise, Myra found herself kissing him on the mouth instead, his lips surprisingly soft against hers. It was so unexpected that she didn't pull away, slightly off balance, and in the next heartbeat, he turned his head ever so slightly to settle his mouth more firmly against hers and was kissing her with satisfactory thoroughness.

Senses scattered, breathless, a little dizzy, Myra put her hand on his shoulder, intending to push herself free of him. But then his lips parted with silken insistence and she started kissing him back without really thinking about it, welcoming the sly touch of his tongue, feeling herself start to slip dangerously near the edge of self-control.

The phone always had great timing and rang loudly. Myra tore her mouth from Kairav's, heart racing, flustered and out of breath. Shaking her fingers free of his grasp, she turned and swiped the green on her mobile. "What?"

There was a startled silence on the other end. Then Shruti's voice, slightly reproachful. "It's Sachin for Kairav, Myra. Something about the project. Do you want me to have him call back?"

"No." Stepping well away from Kairav, she took a deep breath. "No, he'll take it. Thanks." Still holding the mobile to her ear, she stood there for an unsteady moment, not even daring to look at Kairav. "It's Sachin. About the integration."

He reached up to take the mobile from her hand, looking at her, a tiny frown wedged between his strong brows. He then put the mobile to his ear and said, "I will call back, Sachin." He cut the call. Then he looked at Myra.

"We, uh, maybe we should talk about this."

Taking another deep breath, she slipped from between him and his desk.

"This part of the project is your baby," she said carelessly, deliberately misunderstanding him. "Right now I've got loads of stuff to get in place, with my team."

"Not the project, damn it, Myra!"

He looked puzzled and a little unsettled, and suddenly Myra didn't want to talk to him about anything, least of all why she'd been kissing him as though she meant to do just that. This morning's lapse in the kitchen had been one thing, he'd come on to her, after all. So she could blame her reactions on surprise and sleep deprivation. But this slip had been all hers. And there was no way she could explain what the hell she'd been doing without making things even worse than they already were.

Before he could say anything more, she reached across and pressed a button on his desk phone, bringing Sachin Jain on the line. Then she gently took her mobile from his hand, turned and headed for the door as though she had nothing on her mind at all but the upcoming negotiations with Info Capital.

Kairav had his mouth open to call her back, then realized that Sachin had answered the call, no doubt wondering what was going on. Swallowing his impatience and confusion, he ran his fingers through his hair, then loosened the knot in his tie, undid the collar button on his shirt and tapped the speaker mode on. "Sachin! What's the update?"

▼

Something was going on, and he didn't like it at all.

Kairav wandered across his wide, dimly-lit living room again and stood by the windows, looking down at the huge lawn through the light drizzle that coated everything in a wet blanket, each drop trying to show off a rainbow in them.

And as he had about twenty times tonight, he glanced at his mobile on the sleek black glass table against the far wall. He wanted to call her. Wanted her to come over, filling the rooms around him with that special warmth she carried with her like sunshine. And he wanted to touch her again. To fill his hands with her silky hair, run them through his fingers, lower his mouth to hers and kiss her until he was shaky with it.

And that was what was keeping him from picking up the phone and dialling her number.

He lifted the half-forgotten mug of coffee in his hand and took a big sip, barely tasting it. Because the woman he was thinking about wasn't Navya Mehta or any of the dozen other gorgeous and ready-to-sleep women he could think of, but Myra Sharma.

Those few hot minutes with her that morning had triggered an attack of the wants so bad, he could taste it. And while his brain knew that making love to Myra was out of the question, his body had no such doubts.

He glowered out into the misty night and thought of calling Navya. She'd be all too happy to come over and take the edge off.

Except that was just a little too clinical. Granted, he'd pretty much given up on the concept of love, but there should still be more to a sexual encounter than simple physical satisfaction. Hell, if that's all he wanted, he didn't need Navya or Myra.

It made him smile slightly and he met his own reflection on the rain-wet window. Break-up blues, Myra had called it. That's all this was.

He looked at the phone again, wanting to call Myra. Then he thought that actually he did not care about love or relationships. But he started wondering what this strange empty wanting was, that sat cold and low somewhere near in his brain, or was it inside his heart?

The phone rang, probably at midnight.

It always rang when she was least expecting a call.

When the phone rang a little after twelve, Myra simply groaned and pulled the bedsheet over her head. Not this time. No way. He could plead and beg all he wanted, but she was not running over there again, break-up blues or no.

The phone rang insistently again, and she swore that she would avoid it the way she avoided fake beggars on the street, squinting at the clock as though to assure herself it really was midnight.

It was.

Grabbing her mobile, she shoved it against her ear. Actually she wanted to shove it under someone's…

"This," she said sleepily, "had better be damned good!"

The sizzle of an empty line answered her. Then, quietly, a voice murmured, "Oh damn! Did I wake you sweetheart?" A soft chuckle. "I just wanted to wish you our six month anniversary, or should I call it six-monthly-versary?"

"Oops," she mumbled, sinking back against the mound of pillows, eyes closed. "Akhil! Where on earth are you, happy to you too?" Was it already six months, she wondered.

"Didn't you get my message?"

"Message?" Myra rubbed her eyes with her knuckles, vaguely remembering seeing something on her mobile. "Um, yeah. Yeah, I did, I guess. Forgot, that's all."

"I'd hoped you might call tonight," he chided gently.

"Sorry, I've been running all day. I got home late and just crashed."

"Bad news. I'm stuck here for another week, at least. I know I promised to come to you this weekend, but..."

She could hear the shrug in his voice and winced guiltily. She'd completely forgotten he'd been planning to come out to Delhi this weekend. "That's...um...actually just as well. We are in negotiations with an investor, and I'm working crazy hours. We're going to be tied up all weekend."

"You and Kairav? Together?"

She smiled into the darkness. "Along with a dozen or so other people."

Akhil gave a groan. "So let that dozen or so other people take care of things, and fly over here in the morning. You can go shopping while I'm in my meetings, and we can spend the evenings together, drinking wine and playing tourist."

Myra laughed. "It's tempting, but..."

"But Kairav wins again," he said with a hint of irritation in his voice.

"This isn't a contest, Akhil," Myra said quietly.

She could almost hear him smile. "No, I know it's not, sweetheart. Sorry. It's just that I miss you. And it bugs the hell out of me that I'm stuck here, all alone, while Kairav's got you all to himself."

"He's just a friend, Akhil. You know that."

"So you keep saying. But the way you talk about him, I sometimes wonder."

"Well, you don't have to worry." Myra stared at the still and motionless ceiling fan. Thinking of Kairav. Wishing…well, just wishing.

"You sound sad."

"Tired." Myra gave herself a slight shake. "Just tired."

He gave a regretful laugh. "My fault. I shouldn't have called so late. It's just that after four solid days of talking bottom lines and investment rates and stock options, I was desperate to hear your voice."

"I'm happy you called."

"I wish I was there with you right now. Are you wearing that pink silk nightdress I gave you for your birthday?"

"Of course." She'd never taken the gift out of the elegant packing it had come in, but it was just a small lie. "I think of you every time I put it on."

Another lie. She realized, with a faint sense of shame that she rarely thought of Akhil at all.

"If I was there with you, you wouldn't be wearing anything." His voice wrapped around her like silk. "If I close my eyes, I can feel your skin, taste your mouth…"

"I… um… It's awfully late, Akhil. I have to be up and reasonably alert. Maybe you can call back tomorrow evening and we can talk about it then?"

He was silent for a long moment, then he chuckled. "You're probably right. I should keep my mind on business. But before I go, there's something we need to talk about."

Myra knew what was coming. Her fingers tightened around the mobile.

"I know I said I wouldn't push you, Myra, but if we are going to get married this winter, we have to start making some plans. My mother's already accepted you as her daughter in her heart, and we haven't even set a date."

Myra bit her lower lip, wishing she could just say yes and mean it. That she could truly love Akhil as easily as he seemed to have fallen in love with her. That she could just accept all he had to offer and be happy.

Knowing it was never going to be that easy at all.

"Yes," she said very quietly. "I know. But I..." She sighed. "I need more time, Akhil. Not just getting married, but all of it, quitting my business, leaving my family and friends and—" And Kairav, she almost said. I'd have to leave Kairav.

Instead, she just squeezed her eyes closed and fought back the sudden surge of emotion.

"I'm sorry. I'm not making sense, I know. And it's not fair to you to..."

"It's alright, sweetheart," he murmured. "I understand. Just don't say no. Not yet. Think about it. Take as much time as you need. I'll be here for you."

"Oh, Akhil..." The tears caught her so by surprise that two of them rolled down her cheeks before she could even blink. "I'm handling this badly. Thank you for being so patient with me."

"Look, honey, I think you should sleep over it tonight. Give me a call tomorrow sometime, all right? I'll be in meetings all day, but tell my secretary to let me know. Now go back to sleep."

"I will. And, Akhil—"

"Goodnight, darling. I love you."

The line went blank. Myra lay there, staring at the blank mobile screen for a long while, her eyes filled with tears. Damn it, it should be so simple! Most women would kill to be in her shoes, being wooed by a most eligible bachelor. He was handsome and charming and sweet, had a huge mansion in Bangalore and a family-owned super-successful business… and he loved her.

So why in heaven's name couldn't she just be in love with him instead of Kairav, who wasn't in love with anyone!

▼

"Not free for the weekend? And you are gonna be holed up in the office?"

Myra's younger sister gave a howl. Pooja had called Myra hoping to make it to Delhi for the weekend, for some sisterly bonding.

"Does Kairav have a brain cell or two that's still functioning?" She gave a dirty-sounding giggle. "With luck, by now, hope other things are also working."

"Work, Pooja. What else do we have but work!"

"Mmm. Speaking of Kairav, how many men does it take to change a light bulb?"

Myra closed her eyes, waiting for it. "How many?"

"One. He just stands there and holds the bulb, and waits for the world to revolve around him.He would never take a stand, never commit and never take responsibility himself."

Myra had to laugh. "And you think that's Kairav?"

Pooja looked thoughtful. "Not really. He's so focused on UrbanFork, I don't think he's even aware of the world half the time. That's the only reason I can think of why he can look at you for twenty-some years, and still not see you."

Myra just smiled. Pooja had for years hoped that Kairav would one day wake up and realize that Myra was the girl for him. She never failed to speak of it and in hyperbole.

"Give the phone to ma," she said. She usually caught up with family once every few days, but this week had been crazy busy and she had not spoken to them at all.

"How are you, ma?" asked Myra, when her mom came on the line, "How is pa?"

Her mother updated her about some family news. Her father's retirement was on the cards, and she spoke a bit about how she was looking forward to having him at home with her.

Then her mom asked her the usual questions about her day, what she had done, whether she was eating on time, and getting some time for herself. Her father's voice could be heard once or twice in the background and Myra's mom would repeat what he said to her – Tell her to join a good job and stop working in this start-up... look at me working at a bank...getting respect, with a good salary!"

"Maa..." groaned Myra in reply. Her father felt a huge anger that she had left a stable bank job to be part of the start-up with Kairav.

Then, she heard his voice again. "What has she thought about her marriage? Tell her that this time when she comes to Kanpur, I will get her to meet Varmaji's son... he has completed his master's and is now working as a successful banker in ICICI."

Then again, "You should have never left your job at the bank."

Myra had nothing to say to all this and she told her mother so. Soon, Pooja came on the line again.

"How much longer are you going to moon over this guy, Myra?" Pooja sounded serious. "You're nearly thirty, in case it's slipped your attention." Pooja was always Miss Can't-Move-On when it came to topics like these!

"It hasn't, thanks."

"And what about your Akhil?"

"What about him?" Myra muttered.

"Are you going to marry him, or what?"

"I haven't made up my mind yet."

"The biological clock is ticking. I can't believe you're not even sleeping with him. You might be nearly thirty, but you're not ready to go on the shelf yet. Heck, I was reading an article in a magazine last week that said you can still do it right into your seventies, if you take a Viagra."

"I feel so much better knowing that. And there are more important things in life than sex, believe it or not."

"Quick, name two!" said Pooja, laughing out loud.

She continued, when Myra didn't reply, "You should at least be sleeping with the guy, Myra. It's not as though Kairav's saving his body for you. You said that there is a female, what was her name... ah...Navya Mehta! Isn't she all over him already?"

"I know you have a one-track mind, but it's not what you think. Kairav has this old-fashioned sense of propriety that keeps him from sleeping with one woman while he's in a relationship with another."

"But he's not in a relationship anymore, is he?"

That same thought had occurred to Myra, but she didn't want to think about it now. "I work with Kairav; I don't run his life for him."

"But you're still in love with him," Pooja said.

"He's my best friend. Of course, I love him. I love you, too, although yes, I wonder why I love you." She rolled her eyes.

Pooja started to say something, then thought the better of it and sighed instead. "You still haven't told me if you're going to marry Akhil."

"I did tell you. I said I haven't made up my mind yet."

"But you're thinking about it."

"Now and again." She said it lightly, not wanting to discuss Akhil. Or marriage. Or Kairav either, for that matter.

"Do it, Myra," Pooja said quietly, suddenly serious. "It's time you got over Kairav and moved on. Akhil loves you. Grab him and be happy."

"Fashion advice, sex advice and marriage counselling. Everyone in this country can easily give these!"Myra laughed carelessly, not feeling like laughing at all.

Everything Pooja had said was true. But she didn't want to hear it said.

"I think you're missing your inner call.You should quit preparing for entrance exams for a government bank jobs just because of Pa's pressure and instead move out of Kanpur and study journalism from a good college in Delhi. You have a bright future as an advice columnist. Or even better – a talk-show host."

"And you've got a bright future as an old maid unless you get as practical and down-to-earth about Kairav as you are about everything else in your life," Pooja shot back, only half joking. "You are the most 'I-will-never-move-on' woman I know, Myra. You've got your whole life under control, except where Kairav is concerned. And it's—"

"Off-limits," Myra said quietly. "Don't push it, Pooja."

Pooja was quiet for a moment. Then she said, "Sorry."

▼

It was a beautiful morning; the air was like crystal, the sky the colour of a blue Curacao mocktail without a cloud to blot it. The kind of morning Kairav all-too-rarely stopped to enjoy. But he was damned well going to enjoy this one.

He'd picked Myra up a little after seven-thirty that morning and he was deliberately taking his time, since they had enough time on hand.

It had been too long since he'd done this sort of thing, a relaxed drive to office. The past five years had been good ones, but they'd taken their toll. Two major break-ups, among other things.

Frowning, he guided his mind away from that topic skilfully as he navigated his car around a tight curve. The air was spicy with the scent of earth and he took a deep breath of it, feeling some of the tightness across his shoulders fall away. He realized that he was honestly looking forward to wrapping up the deal.

He glanced at Myra. She had her eyes closed and looked relaxed.

Kairav's gaze was drawn to those smooth, round legs again and again, and he wondered how long it had been since he'd seen her in a skirt. Daring to take his eyes off the road, he gave the rest of her a thoughtful glance. Her bare arms and shoulders were shining in the morning sun. He found himself moving into another world.

Did that Akhil ever take her on a drive, he wondered. There'd once been a time when he'd taken Myra out on long drives and she had loved them. He even remembered taking Tanya on one, but she had hated the long drive and had hated being taken away from her work. He'd gone out by himself a few times, but it just hadn't been the same.

And he missed it, he realized suddenly. Missed the long drives, and missed Myra. She was his best friend, yet they hardly spent time together. Maybe it was time to change that.

If she didn't marry that damned Akhil, of course. He was beginning to wish he'd never introduced them to each other in the first place.

Impulsively, he reached across and covered one of Myra's hands with his, intertwining their fingers as he shifted gears. She opened her eyes and looked at him questioningly. Kairav just smiled. "Kind of feels like old times, doesn't it? It's been a long while since we spent a weekend together."

Myra smiled dryly. "If you'd quit getting stuck up with stupid girlfriends, maybe we could fit it in. But your girls have never liked the idea of your spending time with me."

To his surprise, it made Kairav laugh. "Ria always did think you and I had something going. And Tanya..." He shrugged. "Well, Tanya probably wouldn't have minded if we had, as long as it got me out of her hair so she could get some work done."

Myra's fingers tightened slightly on his, and Kairav smiled slightly. "In a way, I probably deserved it. What goes around comes around."

"Playing second fiddle to Tanya's career?"

"Like Ria played second fiddle to mine," he said quietly. The road took a sharp right turn and Kairav had to let go of Myra's hand to downshift. But she didn't draw it back into her lap, and after he'd brought the car through the curve and had shifted back into third, he held her hand that was floating in the air and braided his fingers with hers again.

"She got into a relationship with me, figuring she was getting the perfect guy. I had beat the odds and the company was going strong, I'd just bought the house, things looked great."

"Every girl's dream," Myra muttered.

Kairav smiled. Myra had never liked Ria. And in spite of his best efforts, the feeling had been mutual. "Then you and Vineet disagreed about the business risks you were willing to take," she said. "You split up with your partners, we started UrbanFork and suddenly Ria had an absentee boyfriend who worked, ate and slept work."

"You can't blame her for being pretty choked up. Hell, she was still in college. Everyone was still partying till dawn, dancing, boozing, having a good time. Except us. I was working twenty-hour days, didn't even have time to talk to her half the time, let alone take her to parties. She was stuck back at home by herself."

"She knew what she was getting into," Myra said with quiet intensity. "If she'd paid any attention to what you were doing, she'd have known you can't just—"

"No excuses, darling," Kairav said with a soft laugh. "It was my fault the relationship failed. There's no getting around it. She wanted me forever; I didn't. She wanted a normal life with a husband who was around, and I couldn't give it to her. When she met another guy and left me, it was the smartest thing she could have done. For both of us."

He managed a rough smile. "I don't know why Tanya left me. Things were going good and then suddenly she started wanting to marry me. Man, I got scared, I guess."

"Yeah, you do seem to have trouble getting it right, Kairav."

Myra let her head fall back against the headrest and turned to look at him. She allowed her gaze to follow the familiar territory of his strong profile.

She could still see the faint scar running along his jaw, when he'd nearly killed himself twenty-two years ago, falling off his balcony roof into a pile of scrap. She'd thought he had killed himself that afternoon, looking down from the edge of the roof and seeing him lying there, pale and still, covered with blood.

She could still remember how sick with terror she'd been, how big, even then, the sense of loss. She'd nearly broken her own feet scrambling down off the stairs in the rush to save him. By the time she'd fought her way over to the ground floor and through the lawn to where he'd fallen, he'd managed to sit up, dizzy, and still bleeding.

He'd reached for her instinctively and she'd been there for him, holding him against her, sticky with blood, then, finally, screaming at the top of her lungs, terrified to leave his side. Varma uncle and two other neighbours had come running; someone had called for the ambulance, someone else had called his parents.

An afternoon in the hospital and fifteen stitches later, he was home, grinning that cocky thirteen-year-old grin, showing off the bandages like a war hero basking in the awe-filled adulation of his peers. But that day had marked a change in their relationship. Until then, they'd been next-door buddies, saying hi-bye when they met, sharing adventures and comic books and the occasional soft drink. But from that afternoon on, there had been something special between them, something strong and private that excluded everyone else.

A few days later, Kairav had taken her into the kitchen and had searched through the drawers until he'd found a knife. Solemnly, he'd made a deep cut first on his thumb, then on hers. They'd held them together and had sworn a Together-Forever oath to always be there for each other, to always be best friends.

Smiling, Myra ran her finger down the scar on her thumb. *Together forever*.

▼

They pulled into the parking lot of the office a little before 9 a.m. Kairav was pleased to see that the others were already there. Shruti's little red Swift was standing next to Bhavik's Toyota Corolla, and Sachin's muddy old Tata Safari stood off on one side wondering if he would get a partner for this week like the Toyota got. There were a couple of other cars there he didn't recognize – Kapoor's people, probably.

Kapoor and Ratan would be in by 9.30 a.m. Kairav felt rested, relaxed and ready for battle. He found himself grinning for no particular reason as they walked into the office building.

They were just exchanging some notes before getting into their respective offices when Myra's phone buzzed.

The phone always buzzed when she was least expecting it to. It was a message from Akhil, *"I miss you sweetheart."*

Myra had just settled down, booted her laptop and pulled out the relevant papers when there was a knock on her door.

Ratan's smiling face made an appearance. "Hi, feel like a coffee? Made it early and missed breakfast!"

"Sure," said Myra, getting up from her seat and leading the way to the cafeteria. On the way, she stopped to check with facilities about the arrangements for the conference room.

A minute before 9.30, as they made their way back to her cabin, Kairav stepped out of his office.

"Coffee, Myra?" he asked, indicating that she step into his cabin.

"Oh, we just had one!" she exclaimed.

Kairav looked at both of them, their relaxed stance with each other, and their smiles, and he scowled. "I need you in for a minute before our meeting starts," he said.

Myra told Ratan she would join him in the conference room in a bit, and stepped into Kairav's cabin. The door shut. "What's the problem?" she asked.

"I don't have a problem."

"You don't?"

"Nope. Why should I? I think Nikhil or whatever his name is, should think about that, not me."

"Akhil," she said testily. "His name is Akhil!"

"Did you and Ratan have a good time over coffee?"

There it was again! The question itself was innocent enough, but there was something not-so-innocent in the words, and it made Myra's eyes narrow. "What is your problem, Kairav?"

"Me?" He shrugged, looking as though he hadn't a clue as to what she was talking about. "I don't have a problem."

"Like hell you don't," Myra said. "You've been on Ratan's case ever since you met him."

"He's just a little too slimy for my liking, that's all."

"You think he's going to make trouble during negotiations?" She thought about it, wondering what Kairav saw that she hadn't. He hadn't gotten this far on good looks and charm alone; Kairav had a mind for business and an instinct about people.

"He's just along for the ride," Kairav said dismissively. "Kapil holds all the cards and power."

Myra didn't say anything, simply looking at him, waiting.

"I don't like the way he looks at you," Kairav growled after a moment. "I don't like the way he's always touching you. And sure as hell, I don't like the way he was all over you yesterday."

"Excuse me?" Myra snapped. "All over me? He shook my hand and gave me a peck on the cheek, and—"

"It sure as hell was no peck. I know a peck when I see it. That was no peck."

Myra rolled her eyes. "Give me a break! All right, so he kissed me. I admit it. Bring on the police, dial 100!"

Kairav's eyes glittered slightly. "You like him, don't you?"

"More than I like you right at this moment," Myra told him, getting irritated. "You're doing it again, Kairav. I told you not to do this anymore."

"Do what?"

"Meddle."

She said the word loud enough to make a couple of people walking past, look around in surprise through the glass, into the cabin.

Biting back her impatience, she said, "I don't meddle in your love life, Kairav."

"Does the name Navya Mehta ring a bell?" he asked pleasantly enough.

"I wasn't meddling, I was giving you my opinion. You meddle."

"When have I ever meddled?" He sounded almost indignant. "Sure, I've given you advice now and again when I see you making a mistake. And maybe I've made a suggestion or two, but—"

Myra turned around angrily. "A suggestion or two? I haven't dated a man in my entire life that you've approved of. They're too old, too young, too rich, too poor, they are workaholics, they're worthless and god knows what all. My god, you even had one of them investigated!"

"The man was wanted for fraud," Kairav said with gritted teeth. "And what about that other loser you dated a few years ago? If I hadn't done a background check on the guy, you'd never have discovered that he had a wife and two kids in Kolkata until it was too late." His eyes narrowed suspiciously. "It wasn't too late, was it?"

"I was twenty-seven years old, for god's sake!"

"You mean it was too late?" His shoulders seemed to swell.

"No," Myra said tightly, "it was not too late. The fact that you kept me working until midnight every single night he was in town had something to do with that, of course."

Kairav looked pleased with himself. "See? I wasn't meddling. I was just looking out for you."

"You were meddling," Myra said, turning again to face him. "Akhil happened to mention that someone's been asking around about him, too. There's even evidence that someone's running a financial check on him. But you wouldn't know anything about that, would you?"

She watched him struggle with it, suck between lying to her and putting himself in the line of fire. Finally, he just shrugged, and said. "You can't be too careful about people these days."

"You stink."

It made him laugh. "Hey, what are good friends for!"

Myra didn't find it funny at all. She wasn't going to let him get away with this sort of behaviour any longer. But in spite of her best intentions, she wound up grinning. "I don't know why I put up with you, Kairav."

The door swung open and Ratan popped his head around it asking, "You guys coming in? Kapil is on his way. He will be here soon."

Myra smiled. "We will be there in a tick."

Ratan glanced at Kairav, who nodded.

They picked up their laptops and files, and made their way to the conference room. Everything was set up and ready. Myra muted her phone, then concentrated on pulling up relevant files on her laptop.

Someone from the housekeeping staff entered, pushing a trolley with a choice of morning beverages. Everyone helped themselves.

Kairav dropped into a chair. "Great idea, making this a marathon weekend. We may get this deal with you hammered out completely, Ratan."

"One way or the other." Ratan gave him a smile.

Myra looked at Ratan, obviously picking up some vibration of trouble ahead, but uncertain of what it could be.

"I, uh… Kapil says the two of you set up the first meeting this morning for about ten."

Kairav nodded saying, "Yes."

"So…" Ratan continued, "You like an early start, Kairav?"

"Always." Then he raised an eyebrow and said, "You look pretty fit… you run?"

Ratan nodded. "Yeah, I run. At home I put in about 8 kilometres a day. How about you?"

A pleasant smile. "I go to the gym. Play tennis. Squash."

"And killer table tennis," Myra put in. "Don't let him challenge you to a game; he plays for blood."

"Don't be a spoilsport, Myra," Kairav said lazily. "Let him decide for himself. How about it, dude? Up for a friendly little game sometime?"

Myra saw Ratan's eyes narrow slightly. "I don't play."

Kairav took a sip of his juice, leaned back in his chair and looked at Ratan with fake friendliness. "So, tell me. Have you met Akhil yet?"

Myra's breath hissed and she stared at Kairav disbelievingly.

Ratan frowned, shaking his head. "No. No, I don't think I have. Is he with your company?"

"Akhil?" Kairav laughed. "Hell, no. He's Myra's fiancé."

"Fiancé?" Ratan stared at her in surprise. "You're engaged, Myra? You never mentioned that."

"I am not engaged," Myra said through gritted teeth, giving Kairav a look that should have melted an iron plate. But it seemed to have no effect on him whatsoever. "Kairav is, as usual, quite mistaken."

"I thought you said Akhil asked you to marry him," Kairav said with just the right amount of apologetic surprise in his voice. "Hey, Myra, I'm sorry if I—"

"Look, I, uh, I will just be back."

Ratan pushed his chair back, his face filled with anger.

Myra watched Ratan walk away, then turned on Kairav furiously. "Of all the under-the-belt, underhanded, pathetic things to do!"

"What?" He stared back at her, his expression of foolish innocence almost perfect.

"Don't what me, mister," she shouted, pushing away from the table and standing up. "I don't know what you're playing at, but I want you to stop it. And I mean it! My life is none of your concern, Kairav. So get out, or I swear I will marry Akhil and move to Bangalore and you can just find yourself another trustworthy partner. And another best friend!"

He had gone too far this time, Kairav thought, as he watched Myra walk out of the conference room.

Swearing under his breath, he moved his chair back, getting to his feet. He was pushing Ratan too damn far. This deal wasn't in the bag yet, and if he couldn't control whatever was bugging him, he was going to blow it big time.

He thought about it as he headed for the door. If he didn't know better, he'd swear it felt like jealousy. But he thought he was never jealous and he did not care a damn about any girl.

That didn't make any sense. Why would he be jealous of the men in Myra's life? He wanted her to be happy, didn't he?

Thinking about it just confused him even more. Break-up blues, he tagged it; that's what it was. He'd be back to normal soon. But before that, he needed to get today in order. Get Ratan and Myra back in and their respective teams. Kapil would be here any moment now.

▼

Meetings. Four that day. It was amazing what twenty people could accomplish with few distractions and a clear focus on the objective,

Myra thought with satisfaction, as she walked down the wide corridor to the restroom later that evening. Another day like this and they'd have the Info Capital investment in the bag.

She'd just spent the last hour with Shruti, Bhavik, Ratan and a couple of his people, discussing the finer details of the contract.

She didn't know where Kairav was. He and Kapil Kapoor had spent the second half of the day and evening locked up in one of the smaller conference rooms, working out on heaven knew what.

Myra smiled again as she returned to her cabin.

Thinking about Ratan. He was interested, no doubt of that. And interesting.

Even more interesting was the fact that she was thinking of him this way. If any man should be taking up her thoughts these days, it should be Akhil.

Sighing, Myra began packing up for the day. Akhil. She was going to have to make up her mind about that. Marrying him would fulfil her dreams: a warm and generous relationship with a man who loved her, a home, children. Dreams she'd once hoped to share with Kairav. The only thing that would be missing was the love.

She stepped out, calling out goodbyes to the team. Ratan and Kapil had left. So had their team.

▼

Tired. God, he was tired!

Kairav rubbed the back of his neck and shrugged his shoulders, trying to work the knots free. He and Kapil had been at it all day, and he was worn-out and stiff.

He closed the door to his cabin behind him and walked across to the coffee machine.

He stood at the window massaging the nape of his neck, his favourite cuppa releasing the refreshing aroma of really good coffee. Another few days of this and UrbanFork was going to be on the path to becoming the big boy on the block, fulfilling every dream he'd ever had. Or almost every dream. There were still one or two missing which he still could not realize.

He thought of his two big mistakes. He thought of Tanya. And then Ria. It had been years since he'd last spoken with her. They'd parted amicably enough, all considered, and had stayed in touch for a while. Then they'd both gotten busy with their respective lives and had drifted apart, she with her new boyfriend, and he with work and Tanya.

Parting company with Tanya had been less amicable. They'd both come together with certain expectations in mind, and then had felt betrayed when those expectations hadn't been met. He'd wanted to kick back and enjoy life, have a little fun. Tanya had had entirely different ideas.

He gulped down a big mouthful of coffee. Funny, how things worked out. He'd been on the cover of the *Business Standard* magazine twice, had been profiled in every major business magazine and paper in the country, had a net worth – even before this deal – of well into nine figures.

Yet, for all his financial success, his art was not just in recognizing the cutting edge of the industry, but getting there first, just like Steve Jobs. But he still couldn't seem to pick the right woman. Or make a relationship work. Or commit, for Almighty's sake!

Myra. Too bad he couldn't marry her. They got along great, she loved UrbanFork as much as he did, she knew him better than anyone, including his two ex-girlfriends. Hell, they probably had a better chance to carve out a little happiness for themselves, than most people he knew.

Then he smiled grimly and finished the coffee in one long gulp.

He stuck his head through the door into Myra's cabin and called her name. There was no answer. He frowned. Had she left?

That thought made him frown even more as he walked back to his cabin looking at the incoming mails in his mobile. But his thoughts were on Myra. All of a sudden she had men coming at her from every direction.

Sure, she'd always had a boyfriend or two hovering in the background, and why not, she was gorgeous. Although that hadn't really registered until just lately in Kairav's head. But she'd never seemed to get very serious about any of them.

But now there was this Akhil guy talking marriage, and Myra talking wedding and kids, and it was just getting out of hand.

He thought of calling Akhil and telling him to back off. But he himself was not sure that he would commit to Myra, as he was an 'I-don't-believe-in commitments' type. Also if he called Akhil, Myra might just find out – she always seemed to find out – and there would be some serious hell to pay.

So the best thing was probably just to stay out of it and wait for it to run its course. She didn't love the guy, that was pretty obvious. So Kairav would just wait for her to realize that and offload Akhil. Things would be back the way they should be, just the two of them against the world; and he could quit worrying.

It made him laugh out loud as he looked through the papers on the counter for the report Sameer, the data analyst in Myra's team, had put together on the estimated worth of UrbanFork. That's how he felt some days – he and Myra against the world.

The report wasn't there and he glanced around, looking for Myra's laptop bag. Frowning, he decided to call her and pulled out his phone.

Then, he decided against it. He would go straight to her home and surprise her. He would take with him a bottle of Chateau Margaux 2009 Balthazar, a really expensive wine that his dad had once gifted him. Then they would work on this report and a few others, and he would go home. It would be better than calling her back to office... and he had troubled her enough, making her come to his home.

▼

He reached her apartment block and went up the elevator. She lived on the third floor. Kairav had gone home, refreshed, and brought the wine too. He was looking forward to the evening, he realized, as he rang her doorbell.

She did not answer. He waited for some time. Was she in the bath? He had with him a key to her apartment, but he had never used it. She had left it with him as a back-up, just in case, or for an emergency.

Now, he foraged around in his laptop bag for it. There it was! He let himself in, opening the door slowly and calling out her name.

He smiled a little as he caught the scent of her perfume in the air, hints of aroma and exotic oils and some underlying fragrance that always made him think of long steamy nights, crumpled sheets and sex. It was subtle and faint, but effective as hell. And she wore it half-heartedly often, in his estimation.

Probably just as well, he decided, as he threw his bag on the sofa in the living room, and glanced at the pile of scattered papers on the centre table. It would be mighty distracting to have her smelling that good all the time.

He looked through the papers. Was she at home? He wandered around, looking into the kitchen... then knocking on the bedroom door. Not getting an answer, he pushed it open. The room was dimly lit by a bedside lamp. She wasn't there, but he heard the sound of the shower running. Then his eyes fell on something, something that intrigued him even more. A negligee. A pale pink thing, sheer enough to make him swallow hard. He stepped into the room tentatively. He picked it up, running the webby fabric though his fingers.

It disconcerted him, although he couldn't quite figure out why. Probably because he'd never given much thought to what Myra wore to bed. Had never given much thought to her in bed ... except lately. Lately, he seemed to be thinking about it a lot.

And this negligee? He frowned, holding it up to get a better look at it. This wasn't the kind of thing a woman wore to bed when she was alone, planning to do nothing more exciting than read a book or watch a late-night TV show. For that matter, it didn't look like the kind of thing Myra would buy for herself. Unless...Akhil. The question was, had he bought it for Myra in anticipation, or had she bought it herself for the same reason?

A better question might be, why did he think it was any of his business?

Swearing at himself, Kairav placed the negligee back on the bed and moved back into the living room. He found Sachin's report among the papers on the table, just as the bathroom door clicked open. He glanced at the half-open bedroom door a little guiltily. Through the big mirror on the bedroom wall, he saw Myra's reflection as she stepped out of the bathroom, naked, a towel in her hand.

Her reflection was nothing but a blur of tanned curves in the semi darkness, but he swore and with great difficulty moved his eyes away.

Rubbing her wet hair with a towel, Myra was still thinking about Akhil as she walked out of the bedroom and down the short corridor to the living room and kitchen. It took her a moment to even realize that Kairav was in the living room, lying across the sofa, looking over a handful of papers. She jerked to a stop, her mind in a whirl.

He looked up, his brows moved together. "Is Sameer sure about these figures?"

Wearing only her robe and a layer of body oil, Myra hesitated, then walked through to the kitchen area. "What the f…? How did you come in? And I can see that you have made yourself pretty comfortable on the sofa? Should I serve you some tea?"

He looked at her for a blank moment, then winced. "Sorry. I did ring the bell several times, but you didn't hear me. I used the back-up key I had with me. And yeah, tea's fine, but only if it's the real stuff and not those weeds and berries you're always brewing up."

"Real stuff." She smiled with gritted teeth and popped a couple of bags of a herbal blend into a ceramic teapot. "Sameer's sure about those figures. If anything, they're on the higher side. Even if we get the investment for a little less than this, it would still be fantastic."

Kairav looked back down at the sheet of paper he was holding and gave a low whistle.

"How did your meeting with Kapil go today?"

"Good." A slow smile tipped his mouth up on one side. "Better than good. What about you?"

"I spent most of the day with Ratan and his team, going over all that they wanted clarity on. We had to generate a whole set of new reports. Talk about a nightmare!"

"Can you get a handle on it?"

"I'll get a handle on it."

Kairav's grin widened. "You're not really going to marry Akhil and leave all this, are you?"

The electric kettle whistled. Myra turned the switch off, then poured boiling water into the teapot. "Make me an offer I can't refuse," she said lightly. "I haven't said yes to Akhil yet."

Smiling mischievously, she set the pot of tea, two cups, spoons, a bowl of honey and cinnamon mix on a tray and carried them across to the sofa.

"Maybe I'll marry Ratan instead. He seems quite interested."

"Too damned interested," Kairav growled as she set the tray on the side table beside him. "What's all this talk lately about getting married, anyway?"

"You're the one who brought it up."

"So then I'm the one who's telling you to forget it. Marriage isn't at all a thing to look up to."

Kairav reached across and tossed the papers he was holding onto the table. "In fact, it isn't anything."

"Kairav…" Myra sat down on the edge of the sofa beside him, reaching down to smooth a tangle of hair off his forehead. "Don't be too hard on yourself over this. You made a couple of bad choices, that's all. The next time will probably be everything you've ever dreamed it would be."

"The next time?" He smiled dryly, then slipped both arms loosely around her waist and pulled her down across his chest. "Darling, I don't think there can be a next time."

Myra went still with surprise, hardly daring to breathe. Kairav cradled her against him as though it was the most natural thing in the world to do, his breath stirring her hair slightly, arms folded around her comfortably. And then, after a moment or two, she realized he probably wasn't even aware of what he was doing.

She was his best friend and he needed the touch of another person, so what more to do than to reach for her?

Telling herself it couldn't hurt, she relaxed against his broad chest, breathing in the warm, familiar scent of him, feeling his body heat soak through the robe right to the depths of her heart. His heartbeat was solid and slow and regular beneath her, and she closed her eyes, knowing it wasn't right to even pretend for these few minutes that he really cared. That this casual hug was anything more than a need for comfort, and she was there for any reason other than mere convenience.

"You know what I was thinking?" he said after a minute or two.

"I'm afraid to ask." He was rubbing her back, and Myra slipped her arm around him.

"I was thinking that when this deal is finished, we should take a week off and go on a cruise. Remember when we were in college and always talked about doing that? We never did make it."

"You were practically married to Adi," she reminded him. "You guys spent every minute together, working on your computer and software design. Then there was a long list of your exes – Aditi, and Richa, and Teena, and—"

"Okay, okay," he said with a chuckle, "I get the point. But you didn't have a lot of time, either, with all those guys hanging around you. I remember Dheeraj; he always looked like he'd just stepped out of the pub after hitting on at least ten girls. And—"

"Dheeraj was not like that," she protested, laughing.

"Uh-huh. There was that other guy, the sports guy with more muscles than brains who tried to kill me that night in F Bar."

"Oh Siddharth! I remember. But you were the one who was drunk and started the fight. And who was that girl you were with that night, the one with the huge fake breasts ...?"

"Aparna," he said dryly. "And contrary to your opinion on the matter, they were real."

"I'm sure," she replied just as dryly. "And I don't blame Siddharth for getting mad. You kept telling Aparna that there was a direct link between getting implants and brain damage."

"He had an equally high opinion of engineering students. What did he call Adi? A giraffe-necked geek."

"Adi *was* a giraffe-necked geek," Myra reminded him gently. "He was sweet and nice, but let's face it, he'd wear the same shirt for weeks, he had a long neck like a giraffe, his hair always looked like it had been chewed by rats and he lived on McDonald's burgers and soft drinks, detrimental to both heart and health. I always liked Adi a lot, but he was in another world half the time."

"Well, that giraffe-necked geek's been married to the same woman for ten years and has two kids, so I guess he had something going for him besides an IQ that was tipping off the scale."

"He married that tiny little Garima Khokha, didn't he? She absolutely adored him even back then."

"I was thinking about Adi today. He'd go nuts if he could see some of the research the Info Capital people are into. They've invested in virtual reality and artificial intelligence even before we started thinking about it, and I have to tell you, they're really ahead of us in some areas. Kapil has so many great ideas, all so inspiring. And he goes out to get what he wants. After all, it's all about who reaches at the right place first! How, does not matter."

Myra had to smile, hearing the old excitement in his voice. "What's Adi doing now?"

"Last I heard, he'd sold his app company and was working as a consultant for some other tech start-ups. Wish I could convince him to come on board with us. I could sure use some of that genius he has with coding."

"So ask him."

There was a long and thoughtful silence. "Do you think he would?"

"Sometimes all you have to do is ask, Kairav."

"It'd be like old times." He tightened his arms around Myra and kissed the top of her head. "Adi and Garima, you and me. Hell, we'd be invincible."

You and me. Myra smiled against Kairav's chest, refusing to allow herself to even think it could ever happen. "Not if it means you're going to start beating up all my boyfriends again."

"I just beat up one. Ravi Something. And he deserved it, examining you like that. You were sixteen years old!"

"I'd forgotten about Ravi."

"I caught him trying to kiss you behind the canteen, and I didn't like the way he always tried to put his arm around you."

"He was cute."

"He had the IQ of a donkey."

"Unlike the girls you used to date in college, of course, who were all scholars, right?"

Kairav had to grin. "Yeah, yeah, okay. But for the record, I did date some pretty bright girls, too. Hell, I almost tried to date you for a couple of months, but you're so bright, you scare me."

"Until you threw me over for another girl."

Kairav was quiet for a moment, thinking back to those days. He'd believed in magic back then, had believed in dreams. "Not one of my smarter decisions," he said thoughtfully, kissing the top of Myra's head again. "I should have gone after you that summer. I never felt right about the way things ended between us after that weekend. Maybe if I hadn't been so caught up in that damned app Adi and I were designing, or if you'd stayed in Delhi instead of taking that internship outside Delhi… hell, who knows."

He rested his chin on the top of her head thinking that they might have been good together if they'd given it a chance. But he'd waited too long, and anything she'd felt for him had changed and he'd missed his chance.

"I guess you just don't know what you've got until you've lost it," he muttered half to himself without actually understanding what he said.

Myra didn't say anything. She was nestled against him as though she belonged there, comfortable, natural, fitting into the contours of his body.

Funny, how he'd never really noticed that before. He noticed it now, though, perhaps a little too vividly, very aware of the pressure of her breasts against his chest, the curve of hip and bottom against his lower belly, thigh against thigh. And he could feel the warmth of her, carrying with it the scent of wildberry shower gel and clean feminine skin.

He thought of holding her the other morning, of the feel of her skin, the taste of her mouth… thoughts that led to other thoughts… He had to get out of here.

Now.

Teeth gritted, he pushed Myra gently away from him and sat up.

"Got to go, darling… I just came for these papers…" he murmured, not meeting her eyes in case she could read even some of what he was thinking in his eyes. Because if she did, she'd kill him. Right here, right now.

She didn't say anything. Just nodded, her head down slightly, so her hair partially hid her features. Her robe had come loose so the front gaped a little.He let his eyes follow the neckline down, tracing the delicate curve of her throat, the soft swell of the top of her breast, her skin smooth and lightly covered with body oil…

Taking a deep breath, Kairav leaned over and gathered up the papers he'd tossed aside earlier, trying to get his thoughts back under control. What the hell was happening to him, anyway? It was as though he'd never seen her before or something.

This was Myra, for god's sake!

His Myra. Hell, he'd always known she was gorgeous.

A man would have to be blind not to notice.

But that had never been an issue. He hadn't persuaded her to be his business partner because she was beautiful, or because watching her walk across a room was a pleasure in itself, or because she had legs that would make an old man stand. There were plenty of women around who fit that, if all he'd wanted was looks.

He'd wanted her at UrbanFork because she was his friend, and he respected and trusted her. Because she had a mind that could think. Because she could multitask twenty crises at a time and never lose her cool. Because she laughed at his jokes. Because she made him laugh. Because when he was around her, he felt like a kid again, as though nothing was impossible and every dream he ever had could come true.

Taking another deep breath, he got to his feet. He needed a woman. He was used to having sex. So much time without sex had messed up his mind, no two ways about it. While he was still in a relationship with Tanya, he'd just put his libido on hold, but now … man, now he was even ready to hit on his best friend!

Navya, he found himself thinking a little desperately. Maybe after this deal was done, he'd call Navya. She was best for such weak moments. Myra was looking at him, a little frown between those lovely brows, her eyes searching his, almost as though she wanted to say something, but didn't know how.

And he had a pretty good idea what it was. If he wasn't careful, he wasn't just going to have to find himself a new partner, but a new best friend as well. "Let's call it a night," he said quietly. "Kapil isn't going anywhere…we will all meet again tomorrow. We can go over this report of Sameer's in the morning. Let's get into office a little early?"

Myra nodded, moving her hands into the deep pockets of her robe. She was tempted to ask him to stay, for it was hard being this close to him. In the office, she had her professional persona as a barrier between her and her feelings. But here, the quiet and the loneliness, conspired to make her wish things that could never be, to taunt herself with possibilities.

She strolled beside him as he walked towards the front door. "You never did drink your tea."

"It's too nice for me. I am the straight-up caffeine person and not the fruity teas type." He grinned down at her, then leaned one shoulder against the closed door as though deliberately postponing going through. "You know," he said very carefully, his eyes holding hers with only a hint of mischief. "We, uh, could… Well, for old times' sake, we could—"

"Are you hitting on me, Kairav?" she asked with a laugh, leaning on the wall beside him and gazing up into his eyes.

"Well..." His grin widened. "Yeah."

Myra laughed again, tempted, for one slight moment, to say yes just to see his expression. Instead, she just reached up and took a fistful of his shirt front and pulled him towards her. "Kiss me, you mad fool, and then go have a cold shower and go to bed."

"My pleasure, ma'am..." He slipped one warm hand around the back of her neck, cradling her head, and brought his mouth down over hers more fully than she'd expected.

It was supposed to have been just a casual goodnight kiss, but Kairav found himself kissing her slowly and deeply, taking his time over it, letting himself enjoy every wondrous moment of it. She gave a muffled squeak after a moment or two and drew her mouth from his, fingers still tangled up in his shirt front, her eyes wide and a little unfocused. "Wh-what was that all about?" She sounded breathless.

"Damned if I know," he admitted. Her hair was like silk between his fingers and he ran his thumb up the side of her throat, loving the softness of her skin. "But we could always do it again and see what happens."

"No." Taking a deep breath, she stepped back, shaking her head. "No, I don't think that would be a good idea."

Kairav had the sudden thought that if he wanted to, really wanted to, he could probably talk her into bed. He found himself looking down at her, actually tempted to try it. It would be nice having her warmth tucked into the side of his body, to turn to her in the night and make love to her...

Except he'd have to face her in the morning and try to explain just what the hell he thought he'd been doing. And facing her wouldn't even be as bad as having to face himself with the same question. It would change everything between them, change everything they were to each other, and he wasn't ready to lose her.

"No, you're probably right," he said quietly, leaning down to kiss her again, but lightly this time. "We've got a good thing going here, right? It would be a shame to spoil it with something as self-indulgent and shallow as a night of spectacular sex." He gazed down at her as he said it, half hoping she'd say, "To hell with everything my boy. Let's go to bed. We'll figure something out in the morning."

And he thought for half an instant that she was going to do just that. She stood there, looking up at him with her lips half-parted, eyes searching his intently. It was one of those breath-held moments that seemed to go on forever, and Kairav actually started to reach for her just as she stepped back, laughing very softly, her eyes glowing with mischief.

"Yes, I suppose it would. Best friends are hard to come by. Isn't that what we agreed on?"

Grinning broadly, Kairav reached out to comb a handful of silken dark hair off her forehead with his fingers. "Of course, we could have been wrong..."

Her smile turned thoughtful and she shook her head. "No, I don't think we were. Not that I don't think a night of sex with you wouldn't be spectacular, mind you."

In spite of himself, Kairav had to give a bark of laughter. "I don't know about that, darling. I'm so out of practice, I might just end up embarrassing myself."

"Somehow I doubt that," Myra murmured, soft lips curving up in a sly smile. She put her fingers against his waist and pushed him gently backwards. "Goodnight, Kairav. Sweet dreams."

"If you get restless in the night, you know where to find me." Still grinning, he gave her a wink, then opened and closed the door gently behind him, and headed home, more for her sake than his.

Although he couldn't see himself getting any sleep for a long, long while…

▼

To Kairav's surprise, he did get a half-decent night's sleep, although his dreams had been pretty wet and wild.

And X-rated, he found himself thinking with a grin, as he adjusted the brightness on the screen of his laptop. If Myra had any idea of the things the two of them had been up to in his dreams last night, she'd staple his butts to his office wall. Or use that letter opener on her desk to cut one or some of the important parts of his body.

He shrugged his shoulders to ease the tension across them and leaned back in the chair, still grinning, as his computer loaded in the new program. He was on his own this morning. Kapil had called early to say that he and a couple of his top management team would be in office a little early.

This had never been his favourite part. The endless meetings and strategy, the deal-making, the discussions, all wore his patience thin after a while. He wanted to make things, not talk about them. All the boardroom mind-games in the world couldn't match the childish excitement of watching one of his ideas get to shape, then turning it on and having it work, really work, for the first time.

Myra seemed to understand that. Over the past years, she had taken on more and more of the actual day-to-day details of running UrbanFork, leaving him free to work with design and the idea. If he lost her…

He narrowed his eyes slightly. Maybe he would make a phone call to Akhil this afternoon. Just a friendly little suggestion to back off. Myra would kill him if she ever found out, of course, but it would be worth the risk. She didn't love Akhil. She couldn't love him. He wasn't right for her at all. Too old, too dull, too…hell, too everything!

And Ratan? Not him, either.

The problem was, Myra was just too damn good for most of the men she met. She needed someone who knew how special she was. Someone who could make her laugh with just a look, and knew that her favourite flowers were orchids and that her favourite movie was *Fountainhead*.

Someone who could rub her back the right way, and make her a fresh Strawberry Mojito, just how she liked it, and was willing to spend hours rooting around in musty old bookstores looking for those volumes of romantic novels she loved.

Somebody like him, Kairav thought irritably.

Maybe marrying your best friend wasn't such a bad idea, after all. If nothing else, at least you could count on sharing a good laugh now and again.

Except, he'd never convince her of that. He thought that as far as Myra was concerned, friendship and romance did not mix.

Which was just as well, because he didn't have a damned thing to offer her anyway. Two failed relationships wasn't exactly the kind of thing that inspired confidence. With his record, even Myra – who knew him better than anybody – would be a fool to take a chance on him.

Hell.

He rubbed the back of his neck and stared at the laptop screen, not making much sense of it. Myra should be in soon.

"I have those financial records you wanted."

Kairav glanced around as Ratan walked into the room. "Oh, you are in early, Ratan."

Ratan smiled, tossing a handful of papers down on the table where Kairav had been working. Kairav got up from his chair and walked to shake hands with him. Ratan gazed back at him thoughtfully.

But before he could speak, the sound of footsteps reached them. Both turned to see Myra walking towards them, dressed in a crisp navy blue suit. Kairav admired the picture she made as she walked down the open hall, greeting everyone. And Ratan, obviously, was admiring it, too.

"Are you, um…" Ratan looked at him speculatively. "This isn't any of my business, but you and Myra seem pretty close."

"We are," Kairav said instantly.

"She says you used to live next door to each other when you were kids. That you grew up together."

"That's right." What the hell had they been doing, trading life histories?

"She says you went to college together, too. That you've always been sort of best friends."

"Not sort of," Kairav said testily. "We *are* best friends."

He gave Ratan a hostile look. "Are you going anywhere with this, or just trying to fish something out?"

Ratan just looked at him calmly. "She seems to think a hell of a lot of you. I just wanted to know if there's anything more to it than that."

The question, Ratan's sly way of getting at it, irritated Kairav unreasonably. "Why don't you ask Myra?"

"I did."

Another speculative look.

"She said you're not romantically involved. But…" Ratan smiled very faintly, his eyes holding Kairav's. "I figured you might have other ideas."

"Such as?" Kairav tried to keep his voice deliberately soft.

Ratan laughed quietly, bracing one shoulder against the window frame casually. "She's a hell of a woman, Kairav. To be honest, I can't figure out why you haven't already snapped her up. She's just about everything a man could want in a woman."

"I told you," Kairav growled, looking at Myra. "We're just good friends."

"So you don't mind if I…?" He left it delicately hanging.

"If you…what?"

"No more games, Kairav," Ratan said, with a lazy smile. "I like Myra. I like her a lot. And I'm interested in pursuing it further. I just want to make sure you're okay with that."

"It's got nothing to do with me," Kairav said mildly. "You should be having this conversation with Akhil."

"Akhil… Well, you leave that to me. I just wanted to be sure that I am not crossing your path."

Kairav looked at Ratan with disbelief.

"You don't have to worry about this interfering in your negotiations with us." Ratan smiled again and shrugged away from the wall.

Ratan left then, strolling across the room and out of the door as casually as he'd come in, leaving Kairav gazing down at the corridor. Myra was talking with Shruti now, laughing, completely unaware that he was watching her. That he and Ratan had been planning her future.

Ratan, no way! Kairav smiled. Ratan had a hell of a surprise coming if he thought it was going to be that easy. He'd come in here talking as though it was already a done deal, as though the decision was his and that Myra would just naturally fall into his arms. Kairav knew her better than that.

Or did he?

Kairav narrowed his eyes slightly as he looked at her. He'd always thought he knew Myra Sharma better than he knew anyone. And yet, in the past few days she'd hit him with a couple of surprises, the fact she was actually contemplating marrying Akhil being just one of them.

He thought of Ratan. Thought of Ratan with Myra.

Grinning, he turned away from the window, reaching down to shut off the laptop as he walked by the table. And may the best man win. May the best man win.

▼

Sachin Jain was a new man. The weekend at office, with the small team bonding over the deal-making, had changed him.

Myra bent her head to hide her grin.

She had no idea what it was, but something had turned Sachin into a pretty fair imitation of a polished guy. He was talking. He was laughing. They were working hard, giving presentations and reports, but he was relaxed and having fun. He was even flirting. He was doing something other than sitting in front of a computer! That's the only place anybody had ever seen him in the last few years.

Still grinning, Myra leaned back and watched the two of them. Shruti was glowing like an eighteen-year-old in love for the first time, eyes sparkling, cheeks pink. They were sitting at one corner of a conference table in the large conference room, collating all reports to hand over to Info Capital. Everyone else had dispersed for a ten-minute break, for coffee, for a smoke…

A tiny flicker of envy shot through her, watching them laughing like that. Those first few days of falling in love were unlike anything else in the world – every heartbeat filled with magic, each moment a new discovery, each breath filled with joy. The world became a wondrous place where every word and glance and touch held meaning and tenderness.

It had been a long while since she'd felt that magic.

She leaned back in her chair and massaged the tense muscles at the base of her neck, when another pair of strong arms from behind, pulled away her hands and began massaging instead.

She smiled. "How is it going, Kairav."

"How'd you know it was me?" he asked with a soft laugh, rubbing his nose against her ear. "Could have been Ratan."

"Ratan has better manners than to approach a woman slyly from behind."

Kairav's arms tightened slightly and he kissed the side of her throat. "That's the only way you knew? My timing?"

"And your after-shave. And your smell."

She grinned. "And this."

She ran her fingertip along the white scar meandering along his forearm. "You nearly died in that accident."

"'Only the good die young.' Isn't that what you told me when you came to see me in the hospital? And I ain't good."

He nuzzled the nape of her neck. "I'd just turned seventeen, was half-drunk on Kingfisher beer and cheap Gilbey Green whisky, and our team had just beaten the hell out of the competition. You made me swear an oath that night, remember?"

"I remember." It still made her go cold, just thinking about walking into that hospital room and seeing him lying there surrounded by tubes and wires.

"You made me swear I'd never drink and drive again. That if I did, you would leave me forever." He let his lips rest on her throat for a moment. "You scared the hell out of me that night, Myra. I remember looking into your eyes and realizing you weren't kidding. That if I messed up, I'd never see you again."

"It worked, didn't it?" she teased gently.

"Damn right." He sounded almost subdued. "I haven't broken that promise in sixteen years. But I remember, that day you registered yourself at the hospital for organ donation. Why on earth would you do that?"

"Well, when I saw you lying on that bed with wires and tubes, I thought about other people whose love wouldn't get fulfilled if their loved one met with an unfortunate accident. Because everyone isn't rich or connected. You could get the best health and care, but not everyone can get it."

"Sometimes I cannot understand you Myra, cannot understand how you can be so...so awesome." He was silent for a long moment. "I don't want to lose you, Myra," he finally said very quietly. "You mean more to me than just about anything."

Myra frowned slightly, turning in his loosened embrace, so she could look at him. He looked serious and thoughtful, his eyes holding none of the teasing she'd expected. "Kairav, what are you talking about? What's going on that I should know about?"

"I was going to ask you the same question."

"Meaning?"

"Ratan."

Kairav didn't smile.

Myra sighed. "Kairav, I don't know what's gotten into you lately. You never used to get all bent out of shape about the men in my life. You always meddled and gave me advice I didn't need, but you never behaved like this. You're acting like a jealous husband."

"And you've never talked about getting married before, either," he said with more feeling than she suspected he'd intended. He frowned, looking annoyed. "Hell, I don't know why I'm acting like this, either. Maybe it's losing Tanya, maybe...I don't know. It just seems as though you're the only thing I have in my life that I can count on, and now you're talking about marrying Akhil and moving to Bangalore."

"I told you I haven't made up my mind yet," Myra said gently.

"Yeah, well, if it's not Akhil, maybe it'll be Ratan. And if not him, some other guy." He looked at her for a long, thoughtful while. "I guess I just never thought about you getting married, Myra. That was always something I did." He managed a flash of a smile. "I guess I just never realized until recently that I will lose you to someone else one day. Sooner or later, it's going to happen. And I'm having trouble dealing with that."

"Well, you could always marry me yourself and keep it in the family." She had to laugh out loud at his expression, and she rocked forward and kissed him soundly on the cheek, astonished at how well she pretended it didn't matter. "Joke, Kairav. Just another little joke."

He gave a grunt she couldn't quite interpret, eyeing her a little suspiciously, then nodded towards Sachin and Shruti, who were so absorbed in each other, they hadn't even noticed Kairav. "What's going on with those two? Some problem in my company that no one's told me about?"

Myra looked at Kairav in exasperation. "You know, Kairav, sometimes it's as though you're in another world." She gave a snort. "Not in another world. From another world is more like it. You really don't have a clue sometimes, do you?"

"I don't have a clue what you're talking about," he muttered irritably. "What the hell did I say?"

"Oh...forget it!" Rolling her eyes in frustration, she pushed his hands off her neck and stood up. "I'm going for a walk. And maybe I will catch a coffee."

"With Ratan?"

"If I can find him, yes."

"Forget it." He fell into step beside her and dropped his arm casually around her shoulders, tugging her against him as they walked. "Come with me to dinner tonight. After all this is done?"

"Dinner? Tonight?" Myra stopped dead and turned to look up at him. "Kairav, you cannot just do this. We can't just—"

"Why not?"

"I—" She stopped. "What do you mean, why not?"

"We dated once."

"Well, that was long ago and is history." She thought about it; the idea was definitely attractive. "But you cannot just want me because there is someone else I find interesting."

"That's not the only reason." He grinned at her coaxingly. "Come on, Myra. You're always telling me I work too hard. That I need to take off some time to just have fun. After the deal goes through, we're going to be up to our necks in work. Who knows when we'll get to go out like this. I say we go for it while we have the chance. You were the one who said that life is all about here and now, and not later, 'coz there might be no later."

It was tempting. Very tempting. "Only if you admit that this doesn't have anything to do with the fact that you're just trying to get me away from Ratan."

His grin broadened. "Damn right. You know me so well."

"I could just invite him to come with us," she taunted.

"Just me and you. Four courses. Wine. Dessert." The grin widened wickedly. "Your favourite Tiramisu."

"Tri I Miss U," Myra said with a laugh, knowing the battle was already half over. "You're bad news, Kairav. You always were."

"The worst." Laughing, he turned around and walked out saying, "I am gonna grab a coffee."

Myra stared after him. Where was this heading?

The day went off in a buzz of meetings and presentations. The excitement was simply palpable. The Info Capital team was looking upbeat and by 6 p.m., the nitty-gritties were in the bag. Finally, the team members of both Info Capital and UrbanFork left office, leaving only Kairav, Myra, Kapil and Ratan. The two legal teams that had been engaged in the terms and conditions were putting the final touches to the documents to be signed by the two parties.

It was an exciting moment for Kairav and Myra. After the signatures were done, and plenty of handshakes later, the Info Capital duo left and so did the lawyers of both the firms.

The moment they left, there was dead silence in the conference room. Then Myra jumped up and hugged Kairav screaming with joy. After the first moments of euphoria were over, the two pulled out their phones. Myra called her dad and mom, and Kairav called his.

Myra's mom came on the line. "Wohooo... we got the investments!" Myra said, excitedly. Her mom exclaimed in happy excitement saying, "I knew it! I knew you would do well, beta! I am so happy for you. Here, papa wants to speak to you."

She could hear her mom tell her dad something. Then her dad spoke. "God bless! I am so happy and proud." He asked for some details of how the deal would pan out and Myra told him. Then he said, "Now that you are on top of your career... it's time you also find your soul mate and settle down. Maybe I will speak to Varma ji this week..."

Myra laughed when he said this. He was unshakeable sometimes. Her mom came on the line again and said, "Please tell Kairav, Myra, tell him that our blessings are with you both."

Myra's eyes moistened. Her mom had always, she felt, sensed her feelings for Kairav. Even when some time back, she had told her of Akhil and how serious he was about her, mom had not reacted much. She had only asked, "Does Kairav know?"

The calls all done, the office was still and silent. They could hear housekeeping locking up and checking cabins and workstations. It was time for them to leave too.

Myra's eyes locked with his and Kairav was suddenly thirteen-years-old again and having the time of his life. They'd had something special back then. Still had something pretty special: a friendship durable enough to survive over two decades worth of ups and downs, bad decisions, good decisions, love affairs, break-ups, successes, and failures.

And then, for no reason at all, she found herself turning towards him, lifting her head to look up at him. She wasn't even surprised to find his mouth just there. She felt the tip of his tongue probe the inner circle of her ear, causing her to tingle until she was certain he must feel her quivering. Next, his tongue coursed its way across her cheek ever so lightly, and his mouth came to rest on hers, lips brushing hers lightly, no more pressure than the warmth of his breath. She let her eyes slide closed and put her hands out to steady herself, palms resting on his bare chest. He settled his hands on her shoulders, fingers curling lightly around the back of her neck, warm and strong, yet so gentle... it was almost a caress. His mouth made another pass across hers, barely touching, the tip of his tongue caressing her lower lip to fill her with an intense desire for him.

In the deepest confines of her heart, she knew that he was claiming her with that kiss, in a way in which she had never been claimed before. It went beyond sensuality, beyond the summation of all her experience. She seemed to become one with him, to fuse with him.

Her lips parted of their own accord and he kissed her very gently, just a brief pressure of his mouth on hers, tongue sliding between her lips then away, before she was even fully aware of it. His lips closed gently on her lower one for an instant; then he touched the bow of her upper lip with his tongue again, a silken caress that made her shiver.

Lightly, she ran her fingertips up his chest, hearing his breath catch ever so slightly. His senses reeled as her fingers caressed him, nails catching in the wiry hair as she slid her fingers slowly through it. Wanting, needing to touch him. Tasting the heat of his breath on her mouth and wanting more, touching his lips with the tip of her tongue, feeling them part. Daring to kiss him lightly, letting her mouth rest on his, sliding her tongue along the cleft between his parted lips and finding his there…the first teasing touch, silk on silk, headily erotic.

Too erotic.

It made her dizzy and confused, and she turned her head away, let it drop forward until she was resting her forehead on his wide chest, eyes closed, feeling shaky and suddenly very warm. Wondering what was happening. Why he was letting her do this, why she was letting herself do this…

His fingers caressed the side of her throat, then her shoulders, and she could feel the warmth of his breath on her ear, her throat.

And then, finally, he released her with consummate gentleness and stepped back from her.

"Dinner still on?" he asked. "We need to go out there and celebrate!"

"Yes!" said Myra, breathlessly.

Then he stepped away and smiled. The air was suddenly chilly again.

"Let's leave," he said. She shook her head as if to clear it and began to gather the papers, her laptop and other stuff.

Then he smiled slightly, just a hint of lazy acknowledgement that he was as aware as she was that something had happened in the past few minutes that was catching them both by surprise. Was still happening even as he stood looking at her. Could evolve into something else again should they both agree to it.

The smile widened and his eyes warmed, locked with hers. Then he turned away and started clearing his stuff too. This time, he could feel that there was something different.

Shalom at Greater Kailash was crowded. To the gills. After all, it was a Sunday. Dimly lit, the air was suffused with the energy of a popular pub, Bollywood Sufi music lending it atmosphere. Myra loved the place for precisely this. They hung around till they grabbed two stools at the bar counter.

Myra ordered a Strawberry Mojito and Kairav ordered his regular large Glenlivet, on the rocks.

The excitement of the Info Capital deal hung over their conversation, as they discussed every part of it, analyzing Kapil's cool way of working and Ratan's methodical approach.

"And you know what, Kairav," giggled Myra, "I had one horror moment where I nearly handed him our old report with the other figures, the ones you said to keep off the deal. I had to cover up real fast."

The drinks were served, with some short eats.

"It was a good idea to come here, Kairav. And I apologize for the hard time I've been giving you lately. I keep forgetting you're newly single and not quite out of your break-up blues yet."

Kairav managed a humourless smile. "So do I. Tanya and I were separated emotionally for so long that by the time the actual break-up came through, I had a hard time remembering I'd ever been committed to her."

"Do you think you'll ever find the girl you love?"

Kairav blew out a breath, thinking about the question. "I don't know," he finally said. "I'd like loving someone, and I'd like having someone love me." He frowned slightly. "I'd like to be loved."

"Me too."

Her voice sounded subdued. Kairav glanced at her, finding her staring into her drink. It made him frown, thinking of Myra. He'd never thought of it before. Had never considered her as a wife. "Is that why you're thinking of marrying Akhil?"

She blinked, as though startled out of a daydream. "Yes. Yes, that's a part of it, the loving. The being loved."

"Do you love him?" He asked it straight, watching her face.

"Of course! I wouldn't marry him if I didn't love him, would I?"

But it was a lie; Kairav knew it even as she was saying it. Anyone else would have missed it. But he knew her too well.

"And Ratan. What's he? Just a distraction?"

Myra's head came up, her eyes suddenly cool. "You know me better than that, Kairav."

He winced slightly, suddenly feeling like a fool. "Yeah, I do. I'm sorry."

She nodded after a mistrustful moment, looking only partly mollified. "I could ask you the same question about Navya Mehta."

Kairav had to chuckle. "Now there's a distraction!"

"If you like silicon."

Kairav gave her a startled look. "Like hell, I do, all guys do!"

Myra's mouth curved up in a gentle smile. "Perhaps. But she seemed pretty knowledgeable when she said she could put me in touch with a cosmetic surgeon who, as she put it, 'does spectacular lift-up jobs'."

"She said that?" Kairav blinked. "To you?"

Her smile widened slightly. "Mmm. I guess she thinks I'm in need of it."

Kairav gave a grunt of thoughtful consideration, eyeing Myra's front with more than normal interest.

"I don't think you need it. In fact, I've always figured you had a pretty nice—"

"And coming from a man who has seen many, I consider that a compliment."

"Are you saying I like women with the big ones?"

"I'm saying you just like all kinds of women, period."

He thought it over. "Guess I can't argue with that. God knows, I've had my share."

"Much more than your share," Myra said with a snort.

There was more truth than humour to the words, but Kairav threw his head back and let loose with a bellylaugh, the first he'd enjoyed in a long, long time. It felt good, washing away some of the moody glumness that seemed to hang over him lately. "Can't argue with that, either," he said, still laughing.

Too bad, marriage couldn't be more like this, he thought. Laughing over old times, relaxed and comfortable, knowing each other so well he didn't even have to finish his thoughts half the time. Too bad he couldn't marry his best friend…

As before, he found himself just watching her. He had never noticed until now how graceful her hands were, the fingers long and slender. Or the curve of her bare shoulders in the off-shoulder dress she wore, her skin glowing like smooth satin. Or the soft swell of her lower lip. He stared at that lip, thinking that she had the most kissable mouth ever – sweet and warm and completely responsive.

There was a tiny crumb there now; he reached out and cradled her chin with his fingers and brushed the crumb away with his thumb. Slowly. Loving the feel of her mouth as he traced its curve with his finger again, outlining her upper lip, then down to the moist cleft between.

Her lips parted and he felt the delicate touch of her tongue against his finger. He watched, heavy-lidded, as she took it into her mouth, her eyes locked with his. And it was then, in that heartbeat moment that seemed to last an eternity, that Kairav realized they'd been heading for this moment all day.

He took his finger from between her lips and traced her lower lip again. Then, slowly, knowing there was no rush whatsoever, he lowered his mouth to hers and kissed her slowly.

She didn't seem to be any more surprised by it than he was, 'cause she was sure she loved him. Her lips were already parting in welcome, greeting the probing touch of his tongue with hers. Her hands touched his neck delicately, almost cautiously, one running up through his hair, the other curling around the back of his neck.

He drew his mouth from hers finally, laughing, and brushed her hair back from her face to gaze down into her eyes. "We said this sort of thing wasn't going to happen."

"I know." She traced his face with her eyes, feature by feature, as though she'd never really seen it before. "This is crazy. Let's leave now!"

"Don't you want to eat something?" he asked.

"I want to go home, Kairav. This is not going to happen. I will order something in."

"Damn right, this is not going to happen!"

They settled the cheque quickly. Outside, it was drizzling lightly. They sprinted to his car.

He parked outside her home, in the driving lot and turned to her. He gave her a lopsided grin. "Feels a bit sad to end it this way, doesn't it?" he murmured.

Myra smiled, "What did you expect? A static high?"

She turned, smiling, ready to open the door to get out.

He grabbed her hand and drew her close. Myra did not resist.

And then he was kissing her again, seriously kissing her this time, just letting himself go with it, losing himself in the sweet magic of her. It felt right. God, anything that felt this good had to be right!

"We probably shouldn't be doing this," she murmured against his mouth a minute or two later, her mouth browsing along his lower lip.

"I agree. Absolutely." He lowered his mouth to her shoulder and caressed the soft skin with his lips, his pulse rate all over the peak, willpower slipping badly. She smelled of rainwater and familiar pheromones. He could feel the weight of her breast against his arm and knew he was well on his way to losing it.

"Myra, I want to make love to you!" He groaned and turned his head away, knowing he should be pushing her away from him while he still had the strength. But then his mouth found hers and he was kissing her again, hard and deep, and knew it was already too late.

Myra opened her mouth fully to his, tasting his desire, hot and metallic, knowing she should be stopping him, that this was wrong, wrong, wrong. That she'd regret it in the morning. That, if they made love, working with him ever again would be all but impossible.

There were a thousand reasons, maybe ten thousand reasons, not to let this go on. And yet, she could no more have stopped him than she could stop the rain still hammering down on the roof of the car.

And then he was getting out of the car, going to her side, opening the door and pulling her out by her wrist. They bent their heads against the pouring rain as they ran to the porch of the apartment block, Kairav turning to click his remote to lock his car.

Myra's hands trembled as she pulled out the key to her apartment. It took her a few seconds to get the key into the lock. Once it clicked open, they burst in, impatiently. The waiting seemed just too long. They turned to each other, pulling off wet clothes, almost in a frenzy. She was naked to him, her skin so sensitive that even the weight of his breath made her moan softly. The years dropped away and it was as though those twelve long years had never existed, as though they had made love just that morning, her body still remembering every touch of his hands and mouth.

"You're the most beautiful girl I've ever seen," he murmured, nuzzling her throat, her belly.

"How come we've never done this before, Myra?"

"We have."

"Long ago," he whispered, mouth moving, promising. He captured her lips between his lips and teased it with his tongue.

"Too long ago. I love your skin, like silk. Love the way you smell and taste and feel…"

She lifted his head and kissed him, thinking fleetingly that if she was ever going to say no, it had to be now. But she thought that this night was going to change things, and everything would be perfect.

Everything would be different afterward.

She was truly in love with him. For the moment, he did love her, as deeply and passionately as any man had ever loved a woman. She was in his arms, and that was all that mattered.

And tomorrow… well, she'd try and face it and talk to him. Smiling a little, she slipped her arms around him and simply gave herself over to her true deep love.

And magic it was. He knew her by heart, a conquering hero reclaiming stolen lands. He knew where to touch, and how, and just the right words to whisper against her ear. Knew things she'd all but forgotten, the sly touch of his tongue, the caress of a fingertip, the exact way to coax sensations from her she'd never dreamed of having again.

He nudged her thighs apart gently with his, fingers gently teasing her, readying her, pleasing her, and then, suddenly, he went very still. "Myra..." He nuzzled the side of her throat, her ear. "Myra, tell me it's alright. Tell me you're taking something." He groaned, resting his forehead on her shoulder. "Please be taking something."

Myra's eyes flew open as she realized, finally, what he meant. For one insane instant she had her mouth open to say yes, that she was taking the pill and everything was fine and they could make love, a tiny, tiny part of her thinking of what it would be like to have Kairav's child. Of being able to fulfil even that small part of the dream.

"Oh, Kairav..." She closed her eyes, mind spinning, wanting him so badly, she was half out of her mind with it.

"Don't tell me." He tried to laugh, but it came out as a harsh groan. "Myra, Myra ... this isn't what I want to hear!"

"My camera," she whispered, panting slightly, body so achingly ready for him she was trembling. "Get my camera."

Kairav lifted his head and gazed down at her, his expression making her laugh out loud.

"No, I'm not suggesting we just take pictures and forget the rest! There's...just hand me the camera case."

Obviously thinking she'd lost her mind, he reached around and picked up the leather case from the table to which she was pointing.

"Open it. You'll find what you need..."

Still looking sceptical, he opened the case and peered inside. Then a slightly wicked grin canted his mouth to one side as he fished out one brightly wrapped contraceptive. "Should I even ask why you carry these in here?"

"It's a long story, but you can thank Pooja. She's the one who put them there, for reasons I'm not even going to start to explain."

"Pooja?" He looked surprised. "Little Pooja? Your kid sister knows about things like this?"

"My kid sister thinks she invented things like this."

"Ahh." He grinned, then lowered his mouth to hers and kissed her long and gently. "And here I thought I'd invented it."

"And here I thought," Myra said as she slipped her arms around his neck and tugged him back down against her, "...that you'd just taken a good idea and made it better."

"I have an idea right now that you might be interested in."

"I thought you might. And I think I am."

"Good." He gave a throaty laugh and started unwrapping the contraceptive. "How many of these do you have, anyway?"

"A handful. At least. And thanks to Pooja, in places you would never even imagine."

"That sounds like a challenge if I ever heard one," he murmured.

She wished he would stop talking. Myra's breath caught. "Oh, Kairav..."

The last thing Kairav was conscious of, was hearing Myra give a low, throaty moan at the first intrusive touch of his body, and thinking a little insanely that making love to her was like coming home. And then there was nothing but hot silk and the sound of her sigh, an explosion of pure sensation, as he made that first long, slow, slippery slide into ecstasy itself.

He moved gently and very, very slowly at first, wanting it to last forever, unable to even think of being anywhere but here, so deep within her that they breathed with the same breath, felt the same heartbeat. She wasn't just his for the moment, but part of him, part of everything that made him who and what he was.

She moaned again softly and he braced his arms, watching her with a kind of breathless wonderment as she arched under him, small white teeth across her lower lip as though to hold back a cry of pleasure, eyes closed.

He drank in the sight of her loving him, unable to take his eyes off her as she lifted her body to meet his downward thrust, the muscles in her belly tightening, her fingers clenching convulsively on his shoulders.

Why in god's name hadn't they been like this all along? Why had he been searching for something that had been here from the beginning, looking for the semblance of love when he could have had the real thing?

He lowered himself over her again and cradled her head in his palms. Not saying anything, he simply smiled down at her and a moment later, she smiled back. Then he stopped thinking, stopped trying to figure it out, stopped trying to make sense of something that made no sense, and just let himself go.

It didn't take nearly as long as he'd have liked, any plans he'd had of making it last gone after the first few minutes. It was hard and fast and good, and when he got there first, he was smart enough to just go with it, knowing she'd take longer, that they had plenty of time, that it would be better this way. He didn't rush it, but neither did he hold himself back, and when it finally happened, he started groaning her name with savage satisfaction.

And then, laughing a little at her first look of mild apprehension, he deliberately and slowly took her the rest of the way. She started to argue at first, saying it was alright, that she didn't mind, giving a shocked little gasp of surprise when she realized what he intended to do, blushing and embarrassed at the easy intimacies he was taking.

But then he reminded her it was hardly the first time, and that if you couldn't trust your best friend, who could you trust, and that he was enjoying it almost more than she was. And after a distrustful moment, she let him love her the way he wanted to. And then she gave another indrawn gasp, this one of raw pleasure, and all her arguments were forgotten under his artful ministrations.

It took no time at all, his sly fingers and tongue finishing what his body had started, and she sobbed his name and tried to writhe away. But he held her firmly and watched her ride through it, up and over and down, crying out again and again as the sparks rippled through her.

He wrapped his arms around her, pulling her tightly against him. He could feel the tiny aftershocks still quivering through her and her heart hammering against his as she relaxed into his embrace, spent and dazed.

They lay like that for a long while, comfortable and relaxed, listening to the rain pound down on windowpanes. They made love again, not too long afterward, this time slow and long, eyes locked, not saying a word until near the end.

Then he lifted her across his lap. She laughed, tangled her fingers into his hair and kissed him. And then she was loving him with wild, fierce intensity, her slender body moving like flame on his, uninhibited and joyfully greedy as she pleased herself again and again. Only then did she take the same ferocious joy in pleasuring him, taking along, delicious time to make it so good for him that Kairav had his doubts whether he'd be able to even move after it was over, let alone make love again anytime soon.

They spent the rest of the night like that, UrbanFork forgotten, everything in the world forgotten, barring the two of them and the small oasis of pleasure they inhabited.

Myra got up once and made pasta. She then served it out in two steaming bowls, put them on a tray with a bottle of wine and two goblets. She brought it into the bedroom and set the tray between them on the bed. They snuggled down against a pile of down pillows in a tangle of arms and legs, naked and warm and pleasantly tired, while the rain lashed outside.

Sometime after that, Kairav set the tray on the floor and turned to her with a glitter in his eyes. Then they made love again, slow and lazy, just a prelude to the pleasures ahead.

They took their time, pausing now and again to catch their breath, shifting a little, trying something new, something old. Kairav finally wound up half lying against a mound of pillows on his back with Myra beside him.

He simply relaxed and watched her, loving the way the saffron light from the bedside lamp flickered on her damp, warm skin as she lay there. Her gaze met his just then and she smiled that 'Myra smile' he knew and loved so much. He found himself grinning back, knowing what she was thinking, knowing he still couldn't say *the* thing.

They slept after that, tangled up in each other's arms. Myra half-wakened a couple of times and lay there in the semi-darkness, warm and sleepy, listening to the rain and watching Kairav sleep beside her. How easy it would be to convince herself that it could be like this forever. That from this day on, she'd awaken every morning and find herself tucked close against him. Myra smiled slightly. She knew it was for real and this brief magical interlude would be forever.

So... smiling, she reached out and touched his cheek with her fingertips, aching with love. Wanting him so badly she felt hollowed out and empty, coreless.

It was almost dawn when she awakened again. She sat up sleepily and looked around. Kairav was up, standing by the window of her bedroom, looking outside. She sat there for a silent moment, smiling as she watched him.

She realized how quiet it was. The rain had stopped.

She shivered slightly and pulled the sheet up around her shoulders and whispered his name.

Kairav glanced around, a smile tipping one corner of his mouth up.

Myra smiled and walked towards him. From the window she saw that the sky had cleared and was so deeply blue, it hurt to look at it. She turned her face up to the hot morning sun, thinking a little wistfully that it would have been nice if the rain had continued for a week. Or at least a day or two.

She relaxed against him, feeling his body already start to respond to the promise in hers.

A promise which didn't exist.

"Hey." He reached out as she made to walk by him and grabbed her around the waist, swinging her against him. "What do you say we mess around for a while?" He nuzzled the side of her throat, his hands wandering with deft familiarity. "We could spend the next hour or so doing all sorts of things…"

She caught a marauding hand as it softly caressed her side.

"Kairav," she said a little breathlessly. "You have to have a shower and change and today is Monday. Office time."

Kairav didn't say anything, holding her against him, his warm breath curling around her ear. Then he swore very softly and stepped away from her, his expression unreadable. "You're right. Let me dress and get home. See you at office!"

Watching him disappear through the door, Myra sighed. Maybe she should have just said yes. Then again, maybe not. Groaning aloud, she ran her fingers through her hair, pulling it back. Everything seemed to be so messed up!

Once back, though work started, but people could feel the difference. The chemistry between Myra and Kairav was pretty noticeable, especially to Ratan, who was there for some follow-ups. He was going to be at the UrbanFork office on and off that week. Ratan knew he had lost her, lost her overnight. He could see the love in Myra's eyes for Kairav, the way she looked at Kairav, the way he wanted her to look at him!

He tried to talk to Myra many times, but all he got was made up smiles. She had completely changed.

▼

Myra.

Just thinking about her made him smile. He thought of the small throaty sound of satisfaction she made when they made love. Of the way he'd kissed her inner thighs last night, letting his mouth linger there for a moment or two before going on to other, even more interesting places. Of the whispery little sigh she made when he did...

He had to stop this. Just thinking about it made him aroused and uncomfortable. He hadn't felt this way in years, getting distracted at all the wrong times, thinking about sex when he should be thinking about business. Finding himself in the middle of a meeting and suddenly realizing everyone was looking at him, waiting for an answer, and he'd been so lost in a haze of thoughts, he hadn't even heard the damned question.

Even now, he wanted to see her. Not just to skin her out of her clothes and wrap her long legs around him and make love to her until the sun came up – although god knows that was an idea! – but just to see her. Talk to her. Laugh with her. Be with her. He had never felt like this before.

Hell, it was like being in love.

Myra was sitting at her table, her eyes not quite focussing on the laptop screen in front of her.

And then the phone rang. It always rang when she was least expecting it.

The phone begged to be answered as it rang persistently, and she jerked into consciousness.

Grabbing the mobile, she shoved it against her ear.

"Hello!"

A voice, actually a scream, shrilled in her ears. "Surprise, sweetheart!" A loud chuckle. "I just wanted to give you a surprise. I am here!"

"Here," she mumbled, and shot up sitting straight, with eyes wide open.

"Akhil! Where on earth are you? What do you mean you are here? As in, here, here!?"

Was he really here! She bit her pinkie finger to check that she was not dreaming, and she felt the pain.

"I am here, sweetheart. I got free from my work, travelled five hours, all the way from Bangalore to Delhi, just to spend the week with you. I am at your office reception, please come and get me."

Myra looked at the phone, unable to believe her ears. She got up and hurried to the reception. She didn't want Akhil to accidentally bump into Kairav.

The moment Myra reached the reception, Akhil ran towards her and hugged her tightly.

▼

The smile, the tender memories, the thoughts about Myra, everything stopped. Kairav stood frozen when he saw Akhil and Myra hugging.

"What's happening here?" Akhil let Myra go and looked at Kairav. Now it was her turn to freeze.

Akhil stepped forward and shook hands with Kairav. "Congratulations on your receiving investment capital. It's all over the news. I am happy it has finished and I can have Myra to myself. You will not mind if I steal her for some time today?"

Kairav couldn't think of anything more foolish, as he blurted out, "But we have a team lunch happening today."

"Lunch?" Akhil looked at Myra to see her reaction.

"Yes. Why don't you join in? It's just going to be an unwinding lunch. No one's gonna talk business."

"If that's the only way to spend time with you, I will say yes. But right now, take a break and have coffee with me." He held her hand and waved another towards Kairav, as he walked out of the office reception.

Kairav opened the door to his cabin and stepped inside. He made himself a stiff shot of espresso, then dropped onto the chair and dropped his head back wearily.

What was he going to do?

First Ratan and now Akhil. Men were flying towards Myra from all sides.

▼

Lunch ended in a disaster. Must be all the flying men, but Myra had been pretty distracted. Whether it was being on the receiving end of loving glances from Akhil or the glowering ones from Kairav, it all came to an abrupt disastrous conclusion when she missed a step at the hotel entrance and went tumbling down the stairs. As she fell to the bottom, she felt a shooting pain. She heard exclamations of alarm and one voice, "Myra!" and then she passed out.

Myra Sharma woke slowly. And painfully. Every inch of her body ached. Curled on her side, she found it difficult to straighten her limbs. She released her breath on a short pant.

"Looking pretty foetal, babe," Kairav said as he rose on one elbow. "Don't struggle. Let me help you sit up."

She struggled to remember what had happened. Yes, the tumble down the stairs at the porch of the hotel. Her returning to consciousness in Kairav's car, the hospital, and finally, him bringing her back home, to her bed. A few broken ribs and a wrenched ankle. Painful alright. She was glad to have someone take care of it, glad to be back home. She must have slept deeply after that.

He tossed back the orange comforter, rolled slowly away from her and stood up. Kairav looked down on her and asked, "Pain pill?"

"I can live with the pain, but pull on your pants."

One corner of his mouth cut into a smile. "I want you too."

"I'd let you have me, if I could contain my screams."

"Screams of pain are a real turnoff. I'll have you once you've healed." He walked to where he had dropped his pants and slipped them on.

Myra admired his body. From boyhood to mature male muscle, he was now cut and tight, and fit well in his skin.

"Love the scar on your thumb."

"Oh, I thought you had it too?"

"Oh really." She curved her lips into a smile. "Together-Forever."

"Together-Forever," he replied.

She tracked his swagger as he crossed to her side of the bed, all sleep-tousled hair and broad-muscled chest.

How long had she slept? As she wondered, he tapped her side.

"Let's get you off your side, lay you out flat," he said.

He wrapped one hand over her left shoulder while the other curved around her hip. Then with infinite care, he turned her onto her back. "Can you straighten your arms? Legs?"

Myra tried, grimaced. Her muscles were too tight to comply.

Kairav didn't allow her to struggle. He began a slow, deep massage, starting at her shoulders and working down her arms until her flexibility returned. He then started on her hips. Throughout their years together, Kairav's touch had always been a total turn on. Yet, at that very moment, he healed with those big, strong hands. He massaged her thighs and calves, hitting pressure points that had her sighing with relief.

"You have incredible hands," Myra murmured, her eyelids half-closed.

"Hungry, sweetheart?"

"I could eat a lot, after…"

"After what?"

"Nature calls."

"Got it covered." Kairav bent over the bed and scooped her into his arms, adjusting his hold for her utmost comfort.

He carried her into the bathroom and stood her by the shell-shaped sink. "Can you manage alone?"

"I'm fine. Give me fifteen minutes."

Fifteen minutes took their toll on her strength. During that time, Myra washed her face and hands and spritzed Davidoff Coolwater at her pulse points and her T-shirt as well. She brushed her hair and teeth, each stretch of her arm awakening the pain. Her ankle cast weighed like a cement block. She was pale and winded when Kairav returned for her.

"Damn, I never should have left you alone," he muttered, lifting her against his chest, then returning her to the bed.

Once she was propped against a pile of pillows, her ankle elevated, he said, "A quick shower and I'll whip up breakfast."

Guilt surfaced. "You don't have to wait on me," she said, ignoring the pain in her ribs. "Don't you have to go to office and complete work? I have never seen you take leave for anything." He narrowed his eyes and set his stubbled jaw. "I kind of behaved badly this morning. I made you distracted. And you missed that step. I feel responsible for your tumble."

Responsibility, not love, kept him at her bedside. Definitely disappointing. She forced a smile. "I'm letting you off the hook."

"I'm here for long. Get used to it."

"What about Navya Mehta? The new deal?" she pressed.

"I have nothing to do with hollow girls like Navya. As far as work is concerned, it can wait. Nothing is more important than you, Myra."

Myra felt really happy to hear Kairav speak with such depth. Usually his words were shallow, but not today.

Her stomach growled. "I'm hungry."

"Hold that thought. I feel a bit scruffy. I'll be in and out of the shower in a flash."

He turned, and Myra admired his backside. Wide shoulders, tight butt, strong legs. Her heart clenched with unrequited love. She had wanted him for years.

He was with her now. Taking care of her. Treating her as if she was vulnerable and fragile, and… special. She wanted to savour their time together.

Kairav showered, shaved, and wore his clothes back again. His gaze caught Myra's as he zipped his pants. The sound of the snap was loud in the silence. They stared at each other for a solid minute. Damn, she was beautiful. He liked her a lot. Her natural colour softened her features. Her eyes were deep, the colour didn't matter. Soft breasts and curvy hips. Sweetly contoured thighs. Dainty toes, each toenail painted separately and distinctly from a palette of pinks.

She shifted slightly on the deep pink satin sheets. The hem of her T-shirt slid up, delivering him a flash of all that was female.

He felt the urge to go close, but jumping on her fractured bones was not an option. At least not for a month, or possibly two.

"Cheese and tomato omelette, and toast?" he asked.

"With mashed potatoes and orange juice."

He shook his head, turned towards the kitchen. "You have weird cravings, babe."

Standing before the stove, he wondered what she'd crave for when she was pregnant. The image of a pregnant Myra drew his smile. His protective instinct reared up. He wanted her not to carry anybody else's baby. She could maybe carry his baby. No one else's. But convincing her he'd moved beyond fooling around and had fallen in love would take some persuasion.

Sweet talk and gifts might work. Should that fail, he'd enlist the town's help. Myra couldn't resist her office employees. He'd buy a round of gifts for all those who nudged her to accept his proposal. Nodding, he decided he'd put the plan in motion as soon as possible.

Within thirty minutes, Kairav was serving her breakfast in bed. His woman had an appetite. "Chew, Myra, your stomach doesn't have teeth," he said between bites of toast.

She didn't take a breath until her plate was cleaned.

"Pain pill?" he asked, when she flopped back against her pillows.

"I hate to sleep the day away."

"The more you rest, the faster you'll heal."

"You'll stick around?"

"I gave you my word." He reached across the bed, removed her tray. "I'd like to check my email, attend to some business. Mind if I use your computer?"

"Go in on my screen name."

"Password?"

Her cheeks heated. "Help me up and I'll get you started."

He wasn't about to let her out of bed. "All I need is your password, darling."

She rubbed her forehead. "Memory loss from the fall."

"You broke your ankle. There was no brain damage."

Still, she hesitated. One minute ran into two.

"Myra, it's only a password."

"I've been meaning to change it."

"Change it tomorrow."

"You need the laptop today."

Their conversation was going in circles. "I'll have Sachin drop off my laptop this evening."

"Would you also call Shruti and ask her to visit?"

Kairav nodded, then left the bedroom. For whatever reason, Myra didn't want him to know her password. Curiosity pricked him. He wouldn't press her now, but later, he'd play around, see if he could crack the code.

After putting the dishes in the sink, he brought her a pain pill and a glass of water. She downed both.

He eased onto the bed and took her hand in his, stroking between her fingers. "Last night you started to tell me something, but fell asleep before you finished."

She dipped her head, plucking at the comforter. "What did I say?"

He shrugged. "Nothing much. Just that you had something important to tell me."

"I've... forgotten."

"Short term memory loss? First your password, now words of consequence."

She closed her eyes. "Feeling sleepy."

He squeezed her hand. "No secrets, Myra. I want nothing between us but skin."

"I'll share..." Her jaw went lax as sleep overtook her.

Kairav slowly released her hand, reached for the comforter, and tucked her in. She'd be out for several hours. In the meanwhile, he had phone calls to make. Then, he'd kick back and read the paper. Or, perhaps, he'd watch Myra sleep.

"How long have you been watching me sleep?" Myra demanded, blinking herself awake. She yawned.

"A while, babe," Kairav replied from an armchair pulled close to her bed. His feet were propped on the wooden frame, his body curved deeply into the chair. He appeared relaxed and at home. And very masculine against the chocolate-coloured leather.

"It's so quiet, aren't you bored?" she asked.

"Never bored. You talk in your sleep."

She cut him a sharp look. "Talk, about what?"

"This... and that."

She curled her fingers around the corner of her pillow. "How much of *that*."

"Enough to hold my attention."

She brushed back her bangs. "I must have been dreaming."

"Frankly I couldn't understand much, but I wish I did."

"Hmm," she mulled it over. "Thank god you couldn't understand a word."

Kairav uncurled his spine and straightened. "Is there something you are hiding?"

"Hiding, what hiding?" she teased. "I was seeing a far more interesting dream of a great hunk."

His gaze held hers as he slowly folded the newspaper and tossed it aside. "Hunk, you said?"

"Mmmm, he was good. Better than, probably you—"

He rose in one fluid motion, startling her. Thoughts of her praising anyone else even in her dreams made him jealous. He realized he was really possessive about her. He leaned so close they shared a breath. His gaze pinned her to the satin-covered pillows. "Better than me, huh?"

She curled her fingers into the comforter. "Much, much better."

"I'm the best." He nuzzled her neck, flicked his tongue over her pulse point. As if in slow motion, and with ultimate tenderness, he dusted soft kisses across her cheeks and chin, then kissed her eyelids closed. Time fell away to yearning when his mouth sought hers. He took his sweet time drawing her out of herself and into him. Her heartbeat quickened, her lips parted. She wanted more of him.

He gave her his tongue.

She teased him with her own.

He nipped her bottom lip.

She rolled her legs.

Her ankle fought the movement. Pain replaced pleasure, and a soft cry escaped her.

Kairav jerked back, horrified that he'd hurt her. "I'm so sorry, Myra."

She blew out a breath, forced a smile. "No need to apologize for—"

"Turning you on?" He stood, his back to her, and adjusted himself. "Sachin will be arriving shortly and I'm so jacked I can't cross the room to answer the door."

Myra looked down at her bare legs. "Can you get me a pair of sweats?"

He nodded. "That I can manage."

Kairav's expression remained tight, his steps controlled, as he walked to her closet and found a pair of red sweats in the bottom shelf. His teeth clenched, he knelt on the bed, worked the sweats over her ankle cast and up her legs. "Lift your hips, sweetie."

Myra sucked in a slow, hot breath. Their positioning grew increasingly intimate. Far more intimate than the kisses they'd shared. Her T-shirt had hiked up a little. His face was now mere inches from her bare belly. His hands were tucked beneath her thighs, ready to tug up the sweats. His breath blew warm on her navel.

Steeling herself against the pain in her ribs, she raised her hips, one inch, then two, giving him room to slide the sweats over her abdomen and under her butt.

The warmth of his palms pressed her sides, his fingers pushing the T-shirt higher still, exposing her a bit more. He stared at her. Openly, and with desire. So much desire…

The doorbell rang, and they both jerked. Leaning closer, he softly kissed her lips and then her belly. The kiss on her belly sent shivers up her spine. Lowering her T-shirt, he got off the bed.

"Must be Sachin," he said over his shoulder as he snagged his Polo T-shirt and shot his arms through the sleeves. He walked stiffly to the door.

Myra's spirits lifted when both Sachin and Shruti entered her bedroom. Pretty in blue capris and a tropical print blouse, Shruti set a bouquet of orchids in a glass on her bedside table. From *Cosmo* to *Vogue*, Sachin laid out a dozen women's magazines for her reading pleasure, then handed Kairav his laptop.

Sachin pushed the sleeves of his white pullover up his forearms and said, "We came by to check your pulse, Myra. How are you feeling?"

Myra laid her arm protectively over her ankle and admitted, "I'm sore and bruised, but breathing."

Sachin shot Kairav a keep-her-in-the-bed look, which Myra intercepted. "I'm flat on my back for as long as it takes," she told him.

Sachin and Shruti did not stay long. They checked if Myra and Kairav needed anything else to be done, and left, saying they would be in touch.

Kairav stood up but Sachin gestured that he sit down saying, "We will let ourselves out."

"Flat on your back? Right where every man wants his woman." Akhil stepped into her room.

Kairav looked utterly pained. "Breaking and entering?"

"Two of your friends were letting themselves out. So I took the liberty to enter and have shut the door," Akhil informed him. "I came to check on my Myra."

Kairav spiked a brow. "My Myra?"

Akhil did not react. He truly loved Myra and wanted to be with her and take care of her, but because of Kairav's sudden appearance, he had been edged out. He was really worried about Myra and wanted to be around for her.

Akhil stood by her bed in a crisp black shirt, dark blue jeans, and leather shoes.

Myra cringed as Akhil touched her ankle with his finger. Not that his finger caused any pain, but she saw Kairav seethe with anger seeing this.

Kairav nudged him aside. "Please keep some distance from her, she is in real pain."

Akhil held up his hands. "Go easy on me, dude. I'm here to cheer her up, not make her feel worse."

"Then take one giant step away from the bed," Kairav instructed.

Akhil jammed his hands in the back pockets of his jeans, took a giant step away from Kairav instead of the bed. He looked at Myra and his light brown eyes lit with love and he leaned in to kiss her on the cheek. "Can I get you anything, sweetheart? I am there for you, you know. I have been calling you continuously, but your mobile is switched off. I want to take care of you. Why don't you come to my place? I will take good care of you."

"Sweetheart has everything she needs." The muscle in Kairav's jaw flexed hard. "She is not supposed to move from the bed for a pretty long time. She can't come to your place."

Myra was surprised but happy to see Kairav speak in such a responsible and committed tone, though she felt bad for Akhil. She had never loved Akhil, but he was the perfect arrangement for a well-settled future.

Akhil knew there was no point in arguing. He pressed a second kiss to her cheek and straightened. "I'll be in town another week if you need me."

Kairav did not look pleased over his prolonged visit.

Myra managed a smile and said, "I will try and meet you—"

"Or you may not," Kairav cut Myra off.

"Follow doctor's orders." Akhil felt helpless and let himself out.

Once they heard the front door close, Myra scowled at Kairav. "You sure are bossy."

"You need someone in control when you're spinning out."

"My body's sore. I wouldn't do anything stupid."

"Stupid doesn't include flirting with Akhil? And planning to meet him when you have a broken ankle?"

"I have to have someone in my life. I am about to turn thirty. I need to get settled. You were never there for me until now—"

"Until now…" Kairav eased onto the bed, inches from where she lay. He leaned in, one hand braced on the frame, the other on the headboard. "Remember the last few days?"

She certainly did.

"We're damn good together. Damn good," he said and Myra went still, staring into Kairav's face. He had such masculine features, sharp and defined. His gaze darkened as he dipped his head, caught her mouth with his own.

Their hands remained still as their lips made love. Her heart raced. The rapid rise and fall of her chest was distressing. She moaned softly.

Kairav's chest heaved as he pulled back. He ran his hand through his hair, got his pulse under control. "We need to find an activity that doesn't hurt you or me."

"I never hurt you. It's you who doesn't care. I wouldn't leave you for anything. Would you let me go?"

Her heart nearly stopped. Had she spoken her question out loud? Apparently she had, given Kairav's thoughtful expression and the sudden tightness in his shoulders.

His words came slowly. "We're friends, babe. Friendship lasts forever."

"Isn't our relationship deeper now?"

"That only enhances our friendship." He pressed a kiss to her forehead. "I care for you, Myra. Always have, always will."

She turned her head into her pillow, fought a yawn. "I care back."

"Tired?" Kairav asked.

"A little. But I'm not ready to nap just yet."

"What would you like to do? Watch television, listen to music, read a magazine?"

She didn't miss a beat. "I'd like you to paint my toenails."

Kairav looked at her cute little toes. "They're already painted."

"I change the colour every day."

"You're kidding me, right?"

"Colour makes me feel alive," she explained. "My toes are in the mood for purple, just like the black currant ice cream."

"You want me to put colours on your toes?"

"You catch on fast, Kairav."

"I've never painted a woman's toenails."

"Virgin pedicure artist. Let me break your virginity. Let me be your first."

He gave his head a small shake and muttered, "What a man does for his woman!"

His woman? Was it a slip of the tongue or was it his heart's voice? He wondered about it.

"Nail polish remover, cotton balls, clipper, and file are in the dressing cabinet, along with the purple nail paint."

He returned with the supplies and eased onto the bed. He drew one of her feet onto his lap. She wiggled her toes.

"Hold still," he gritted out, then went to work on her toes.

Myra watched Kairav through half-closed lids. Dedicated to the task, he removed the day-old polish, then pressed cotton balls between her toes. Clipped and filed. Then painted.

"The polish goes on my nail," she reminded him, feeling a drip on her toe.

He grunted, reached for the polish remover, and started over. He clenched his jaw in concentration. "Your toenails are so tiny."

His hands were so big. The brush on the polish vanished between his fingers as he painted on her toes. He was really bad at it.

She wiggled her toes a second time.

"Not now, Myra."

Wiggle. Wiggle. Wiggle. Wiggle.

He grabbed her ankle. "Babe."

"I want to play."

"I thought you wanted your nails painted."

"I want you more."

"You can't have me until your ankle heals." He finished painting the toes somehow, then set both feet away from him and stretched. "You rest, I'll be at my laptop."

Her eyelids drooped. "Stay close."

"I won't leave you. Promise."

He had said the magical words that she wanted to hear. Though he didn't say it in the context she wished he would.

"Myra?"

He was greeted by silence.

Where the hell had she gone? Kairav wondered as he stormed through her house. He'd left specific instructions for her to sit tight, not to go out anywhere with a broken ankle. But Myra had awakened that morning with a craving for a good coffee and agreed to meet Akhil.

Kairav checked outside. Myra's Amaze had been parked outside the house. But there was no one in the house. Myra must have sweet-talked a ride. The woman had no business being out of bed. She needed to rest to heal.

The sexy scent of Elizabeth Arden 5th Avenue perfume drew him to the kitchen. There, he found a yellow Post-it stuck to a clay pot with sprigs of fresh mint. *Breakfast with Akhil.*

Kairav wadded up the note and tossed it into the trash can. His temper spiked.

Damn stubborn girl.

Kairav stepped out and sat in his car and purposely pushed the speed limit to get to Café Coffee Day, Dhaula Kuan. He knew Myra loved that place. It was the only open-air café in Delhi. Since their college days, it was their favourite place. It had a small flea market and an Archies gallery adjacent to it. It was always fun to see her buying accessories at the flea market or browse through giftables at the Archies gallery. He stopped his car outside the Cafe and the security guard saluted him with a smile.

He faked a smile and looked up the steps of the cafe. Taking several deep breaths, he tamped down his temper, not wanting to accuse or alienate her for ignoring doctor's orders.

He wanted to be calm when he found her.

His calm lasted all of ten minutes.

Myra sat with Akhil at a wicker table with high-backed wicker chairs. She'd dressed quickly in a hot pink top and a black skirt. A pair of black leggings and one pink flip-flop completed her outfit.

Sunshine patterned the walls in a kaleidoscope design. All the colour in the world couldn't hide her pale profile. Her lips were tightly set in a small smile as she sipped her coffee from a white china cup.

Akhil, on the other hand, wore a white Polo T-shirt and blue denims. The man chatted away animated, utterly charmed by her presence.

Kairav glanced at his watch. He'd give them ten minutes before escorting Myra home.

The café was packed as it was a Sunday morning. The scent of chocolate chip cookies permeated the air. The edges were black and crunchy, the centres doughy. The less-than-icy frappuccinos were topped with dancing whipped cream.

Kairav edged around a small promotion counter of a new gaming app. A young man was trying out the game on one of the tablets on display, hosting it at the counter. A tall girl wearing a branded black T-shirt was managing the kiosk. Their eyes connected briefly and she took him in. All of him. "Sir, would you like to try the new cricket game?" Her husky voice was accompanied by a tentative smile.

He shook his head. "Sorry. I'm already in the middle of a game."

The game of his life. Innings passed with the speed of light. He had to find the proper time and place to propose to Myra Sharma before he lost her to Akhil. He knew that Myra wanted to settle down. She even had a lot of family pressure, with her father wanting her to marry someone in Kanpur.

As if by sixth sense, Myra turned slightly and looked up. Their gazes locked across the crowded café.

He glared and her smile faltered.

She swallowed hard and swivelled back towards Akhil.

Kairav crossed the cafe and came up behind Myra. Curving his hand over her shoulder, he squeezed. "Time for a pain pill," he said, keeping his voice level.

Her hand shook as she took her last sip of coffee. The cup clattered on the saucer. "I'm ready to leave."

Akhil stood and volunteered, "I'll drive her home."

"I've got it covered," Kairav returned evenly.

"Breakfast tomorrow, Myra?"Akhil looked hopeful.

Kairav shook his head. "Tomorrow's too soon."

Myra pushed herself off her chair, balanced on her broken ankle, and winced. "Two weeks of breakfasts, Akhil, if you let me slide a few days."

Akhil beamed. "Definitely a deal."

Taking her by the hand, Kairav drew her through the crowd. The clumping sound of her cast echoed on the tiled floor. One step beyond the café and into the alley, and she folded against him.

"I hurt like hell," she moaned against his chest.

"Good."

She punched him in the arm. A puny little hit. "Mad at me?"

"I ought to beat you, babe, for sneaking out of the house."

"I had no plans. I just had a big coffee craving in the morning, I swear. Akhil called right at that point of time. So I agreed to have coffee without thinking about the consequences. I even left you a note."

"Consequences caught up with you?"

"I am feeling all broken up."

"Let's get you home." He gently turned her towards his car. Once she was comfortably seated, he kissed her on her forehead.

She dropped her head against the soft leather and closed her eyes. "Thanks for coming after me."

"Did you think I wouldn't?"

"You're taking on a lot of responsibility for a rebound lover."

He wanted the responsibility of being her husband. "I like taking care of you."

"I like you taking care of me."

Silence slipped in behind her words. Myra didn't open her eyes until they reached her house.

"I'm hungry," she admitted when he'd cut the engine. "I sipped a hazelnut cappuccino at the café, but didn't eat."

"There's a bag of cream cake in the kitchen," Kairav reminded her. "Unless you'd rather have an omelette or a French toast."

"I'll go with the cream cake."

He stripped her down and she crawled back into bed. All snug in a long T-shirt. Returning from the kitchen, he produced a cup of black coffee and a bag of cream cake on a wooden breakfast tray. He pulled up the leather armchair and watched her attack the cake.

Within seconds, cream oozed out and smeared her upper lip. Kairav wanted to taste both her and the cake.

He stared at her mouth. "Can I have a bite?"

She set the tray to one side. "Take a big bite."

Kairav bit. Taking her lip between his teeth, he licked, enjoying his own breakfast. She tasted of vanilla cream. And sweet Myra. He'd never tasted anyone so good.

Myra let him taste her. Kairav remained hungry long after he'd licked the cream from her lips. His mouth angled over hers, their tongues tangling, all the while feeding her hunger as much as his own.

She curved her hand around his neck, and the muscles in his shoulders strained at the frustration of wanting her, yet being unable to take her. Her fingers stroked those shoulders, then slid into his hair. All thick and clean and soft to her touch.

She could touch this man forever.

His hand skimmed her body, over her breast, across her bare bottom, lingering on her thigh before finally settling on her hip. Where he squeezed hard. "Frustrated?" she breathed against his lips.

"I'm so—" He really wanted her, but stopped, considering her health.

Myra rested her forehead against his, lowered her lashes. She was hardly able to breathe.

"Time to stop. Before I embarrass myself like a sixteen-year-old."

"It could be weeks."

"We'll wait, babe."

"If you change your mind," she rubbed her hands together, "… you know where to find me."

He shifted on the chair and crossed one ankle over his knee.

"A little conversation," she said.

"Cover yourself with the bedsheet first," he stated. "You're damn distracting."

She complied, tucking the ends beneath her naked bottom and thighs.

"What's on your mind?" he asked.

"Did you see Sachin and Shruti when they came home that day?"

Kairav nodded. "Yes, I did. Why?"

She grinned. "Shruti had a hickey."

"Sachin left his mark."

"Any sign of Navya Mehta? You miss her?"

"I told you earlier too. She is not my type."

She licked her lips and dared, "What's your type?"

He blinked, momentarily taken aback by her question. It took him several seconds to respond. "You know me better than any other girl, darling. You know what I like."

She grabbed a magazine off the side table and flipped through the pages. "There's paper and pen in the drawer. Let's take a *Cosmo* quiz."

Kairav visibly flinched. "Too girly. Real men don't take *Cosmo* quizzes."

Myra located the quiz. "It's on compatibility."

"Girls take these quizzes far more seriously than guys do."

"Let's take it for fun."

"I'd rather poke my eye with a fork."

"Plastic or sterling silver fork?"

"Any fork, Myra. I don't want to play."

"Please..."

Damn. She had him. One simple word, said so sweetly. Her eyes all wide and her lips a little pouty. He was a total sucker for this girl.

"Heal fast, daring. I'm only taking one quiz during your recovery." That said, he searched the side table drawer for paper and pen. He found a coffee cup-shaped notepad and a blue marker.

Myra chose a pink glitter pen to check off her answers in the magazine, then she began to read. "First question we mark separately. It's on body type. How do you like your girl? a) brainless and busty, b) smart and sassy, c) flat chest and boyish hips, d) pouty and dewy."

Kairav rolled his eyes and shook his head. He wrote down a letter and nodded towards the magazine. "Read your choices."

"What letter do you think I picked?" he asked.

"I went with 'D'."

Pouty and dewy? Maybe she didn't know him as well as she thought.

"A person with a desk job ages faster than an athlete," he explained, perfectly serious. "A much younger wife can pick up the sexual slack, ride astride, when my body aches and my knees give out in my golden years."

Myra went still. She was no sweet young thing. She'd wanted to grow old with this man, but apparently he was looking for a child bride.

She stared at him. Stared hard, until his smile broke and his laughter rolled over her, gut deep and husky. Holding up his paper, he pointed to the "B" penned and traced several times over. He'd gone with smart and sassy. "Gotcha." Amusement lit his gaze. "You're so gullible."

"You're not that funny," she sniffed.

"About as funny as this quiz."

"It gives us something to do."

"I'd rather watch you sleep."

"I'll take a pain pill once we finish."

"Sure you don't want it now?"

"Question two." Ignoring him, she read on. "First Impressions. Do you note a) eyes and hair, b) smile and attitude, c) style of clothing, d) can't form an impression until I see the person naked."

Kairav marked a letter, then said, "'C'. You have your own style. Flamboyant and free. I do, however, like you best in nothing but your skin."

"'B' for me." She tapped her glitter pen on the magazine page. "I've always loved your smile. The sensual twist of your lips. Your arrogance grew on me."

His brows drew together. "I'm never arrogant."

"You were cocky as hell in college."

He indolently rolled his tongue into his cheek. "Hard to believe."

She returned to the quiz. "Say it with: a) flowers, b) chocolate, c) concert tickets, d) sex."

"How about all of the above?"

"Pick one."

"Fine. 'D'."

"Ditto."

His gaze turned hot, his lips parted slightly. "Glad we agree."

"Next question, Foreplay: a) gazing deeply into your partner's eyes, b) sex talk, c) soft, sweet kisses, d) sharing a six can pack of beer, no burping."

Kairav drew his hand down his face. "Who in this world thinks up these questions?"

"Write down your answer."

He did. "'C'."

Myra hesitated. "I like it when you talk sexy to me."

"I love your taste," he told her in a deep, dark voice that slid over her.

The man had a way with words. She fanned her face and swallowed hard, barely able to continue. "I prefer sex: a) in the morning, b) at noon, c) at night, d) once a month."

He immediately answered, "e – every hour."

"Any questions that don't relate to sex?" he asked.

She scanned down the quiz. "Favourite vacation spot: a) beach, b) hill stations, c) hustle bustle metros, d) heritage cities."

"'B'," Kairav said, as he jotted down the letter. "I like to go and explore on hill stations."

"While I'm spreading on massage oil in Goa."

He changed his mind and his answer. "Actually Goa is better, as long as I can spread the oil all over your body."

"Dinner Date," Myra moved on. "a) Indian, b) Italian, c) Chinese, d) South Indian."

"Sweet and sour chicken."

"You said that 'cause you know that's my favourite."

"Did I score extra points?"

"A few. But I know you like Italian more." She returned to the quiz. "Two more questions to go. Afternoon entertainment: a) movie, b) shopping, c) athletic event, d) couch potato."

"I spend three-fourths of my life at office. If given a chance, couch potato will be my choice."

"Baking, drinking coffee, and reading aren't even a choice in this question." She sighed. "Moving on. Last question: Marriage plans." She noticed that Kairav grew tense.

His male radar was on full alert. "a) in one month, b) six months, c) one year, d) not in this lifetime."

He slowly crumpled up his paper, tossed the blue marker back in the drawer, and stood. He was trying to act nonchalant, yet Myra knew Kairav and his tics. His eye twitch claimed him cornered.

She closed the copy of *Cosmo* and balanced it on the other books on the side table. "Silly quiz, means nothing—"

"I'd marry the girl I love tomorrow."

The girl I love.

Myra's heart stopped. Commitment wasn't in Kairav's dictionary, she had thought.

Silence filled the room as he snagged her breakfast tray off the bed and went for her pain pill. When he returned, she said softly, "Thanks for taking the quiz."

"It was a compatibility test. Rebound lovers don't exactly qualify for husband material." He paused. "Do they?"

"Depends if he has the qualities I'm seeking."

"Nudge, nudge." He appeared curious about her ideal man.

"Someone who understands that a wedding ring gives as much freedom as it does security. Someone who understands my quirks and craziness and is around when I need him."

"I'm here when you need me, darling."

"I'm talking forever."

Rebound to forever. Kairav needed to say his piece, stake his claim. Quickly.

"Pain pill, please." Myra's request cut off his confession.

His window of opportunity slammed shut.

"Right here." He handed over her medicine and a glass of water.

Once the pill was swallowed, she patted the bed. "Lie with me?"

"Sure." He'd never taken so many naps, been so well-rested. Lying with Myra was pure pleasure.

Removing his shirt and shoes, he crawled up beside her. She rested her head on his shoulder and closed her eyes. When he felt her body go lax, he kissed her forehead. "I love you, Myra Sharma." Then he tested the words in the silence, words he'd been waiting to say. "Marry me."

She stirred ever so slightly. Her lips moved, her speech a bare whisper as she spoke in sleep. "Tomorrow too soon?"

▼

"Any plans for Tuesday?" Kairav asked Myra following her two-hour nap. Any chance she remembered accepting his proposal?

Apparently not. "Nothing for tomorrow," she said slowly, squinting, as if trying to remember something she'd forgotten. "Don't forget to bring me Haagen Dazs ice cream later today."

She placed a soft kiss on his shoulder. "Maybe I could ride along—"

"Maybe not."

She nipped him then. "I've got bored sitting at home."

Myra was restless. Not a good sign. Kairav rubbed her hands. "I don't want you to overdo. The doctor ordered you to relax—"

"I'm sleeping fifteen hours a day."

"If I take you with me, will you promise to stay in bed all day tomorrow?"

"M-mmm, maybe."

Not good enough. "What plans have you made?"

She dipped her head. "Maybe go to office for a few hours."

"No way in hell."

"You're not my boss."

"I am not, but I am bossy."

She rose on one elbow, winced, eased back down, and wrinkled her nose. "So am I.But I'll stay."

Then she said, "Can I have clean sheets too?"

He could change a bed. "No problem."

"Will you do a load of laundry?"

He could separate whites from colours. Delicates from denim.

"Water my plants?"

Also doable.

"Maybe you could do some dusting." Myra hated housework.

"I don't do windows."

"Neither do I."

Kairav pointed towards the bed. "Sit tight. I'll be right back."

Sit tight didn't register in Myra's brain. A plastic bag in hand, he returned from the kitchen to find her hung up on the bed frame, one arm and one leg dangling limply over the side. She was flat out stuck. "You moved," he accused.

"Getting in is much easier than getting out," she huffed.

"You need my help." He stood several feet from the bed, crossing his arms over his chest. "I should leave you in that position. You wouldn't go far."

Myra struggled, then quit the fight. "Don't be a jackass."

"Jack who? Getting a little testy, babe?"

"Prepare to die when I'm back on my feet."

"I'm scared. I'll be looking over my shoulder, my knees shaking for four weeks." She went quiet on him. Her face was buried between the bed mattress and the bed frame. "You okay?"

Her voice was muffled. "I'm plotting your torture."

"Silken bonds and feather whips?"

"Knife and leather hunter."

The girl was vicious. Threats of castration sent him to her side. Tucking one hand beneath her shoulder and one behind her knees, he gently lifted her against his chest. She glared at him all the way to the bathroom. She was ticked off, and when he set her down, he tucked her into his body and kissed away her anger. He carefully moved her to the leather armchair.

He stepped back, and with two strong tugs, stripped the bed of its sheets. Rustling through her linen closet, he selected navy satin. The last time he'd lain on sheets like that, the bed withstood a full night of motion. They had invented positions, making love until exhaustion forced them to sleep.

He turned down the bed and settled Myra on the clean sheets. She sat resting on two pillows. "I need to talk to you, Kairav."

"We are talking Myra, aren't we?"

"Why are you doing all this for me?"

"As a friend, it's my responsibility to take care of you."

Friend, responsibility, is that all she was? Myra felt pain, not because of the internal wounds or broken ankle, a pain from deep down her heart. After all this time they had shared, Kairav still just takes me as a friend, as a responsibility. She needed a secure future, she needed someone who would be there by her side, for ever and ever. Maybe it wasn't worth waiting for Kairav anymore.

Breaking her thoughts, Kairav said, "I know you need me sweetheart."

"Yes, I need you, I always have. But do you need me?"

"Personally and professionally, you have always been there for me. Whether it was supporting me in my break-ups or the big Info Capital deal, I couldn't have done it without you. I really want you, Myra."

"You want me, but you don't need me. I know you've never quite understood the difference, but you'll figure it out soon. When I'll be out of your life, probably then you would understand." She had taken her big step right now, but Kairav didn't realize it.

"Out of my life?" He said it dryly, pulling the armchair closer to the bed. "I don't think you mean that."

"I mean everything I said." She smiled very slightly, but there was a distinct chill to it.

He just stared at her, not smiling now. Knowing she didn't mean it, but not appreciating the joke.

Myra faked a yawn. "I'm really tired, and ready for bed."

The bed was good. It could hold her, get her feelings off her chest. She needed to see where things stood between them. Do or die.

Myra felt a reminder ringing, a reminder which no single girl would want, a reminder that she would die alone, until the cats found her.

She was reminded, again, of her favourite movie, *When Harry Met Sally*, and the lines she thought applied to her in particular: "Suppose nothing happens to you. Suppose you live out your whole life and nothing happens. You never meet anybody, you never become anything, and finally you die one of those New York deaths which nobody notices for two weeks until the smell drifts into the hallway."

Not that she was from New York; she was from Kanpur, born and bred.

But the rest of it applied to her. And she decided not to let it happen.

Myra thought of Kairav – how she'd snuck out of the house when he'd stepped out to get some things, including the ice cream. He wanted her to rest. She'd wanted to move out of this non-committed web in which she was tangled.

When Kairav discovered her gone, there would be hell to pay. She booked an Uber and a car came around double quick.

If she could just stop crying, damn it, everything would be fine. Myra gritted her teeth and battled against a fresh flood of tears, refusing to give in.

Poor Akhil. He was looking frazzled and harried and worried half to death.

This had to stop. She had to get a grip on herself. She had a life to plan. A life with someone who loved her. A life with someone who would be there forever. A life with Akhil. She had left home and called him. She had accepted his long-awaited marriage proposal. She was angry with Kairav and knew he would never commit. She wasn't even sure if he loved her.

Kairav entered the room with Haagen Dazs ice cream served out in a bowl in his hand, blueberry cheese ice cream, her favourite, only to find the bed empty. He checked the bathroom. She wasn't there.

"I leave her for a few hours and she goes away on her escapades." He walked back into the kitchen, towards the refrigerator to check if she had left a note. He found one paper nicely folded and stuck behind the magnetic bottle-opener stuck on the door. He kept the ice cream inside to keep it cold, but what he was going to read was going to run chills down his spine.

He unfolded the paper casually but hurriedly.

Dear Kairav,

I want to thank you for being there with me this week and taking care of your best friend. Thanks for being such a responsible and caring.friend I never expected this from you. It was always me who was there for you. For your college assignments, your office work, your family problems and even your break-ups.

I've been through your break-ups many more times than I can count already. Aditi. Ria. Tanya. And all the others, all your in-between girlfriends. Well, no more. Good old Myra isn't taking it anymore. I am out of here.You're on your own.

I'm going to marry Akhil. I've already called him and told him I'll be with him.

I know you won't understand, Kairav. And I guess that's the real reason I'm leaving.

Love,

Myra

Something went through Kairav like a sword blade, ice-cold and deadly and right through the heart. He forgot to breathe for a moment or two, his mind wheeling with the enormity, the impossibility, of what he had just read.

He took a deep breath. Then another. It was very quiet. Too quiet. As though all the energy and life had been drained from the world. He could hear the clock on the wall behind him ticking. Could hear, faintly, the sound of traffic on the street below. Voices, far away. Unimportant. The sound of his own heart beating, echoing in the emptiness his life had just become.

He felt oddly hollow. As though he were merely a shell of someone he'd once been, the core of him gone, nothing left but the outer wrappings. He thought, fleetingly, of the investment they had just gotten. Of how hard it was going to be without her.

Without her.

It wasn't possible, of course. She'd get halfway and realize she'd overreacted and would be back up here, a bit embarrassed, laughing about it. And it would be like old times again. Just him and Myra against the world.

It made him feel better, thinking it through like that. He sat down and started reading the letter again. But none of it made much sense. He kept looking at the door.

But no one came through, and he told himself he was being stupid.

She'd be back. She had to come back. She was his best friend. And best friends didn't just leave like that.

But she didn't come back.

He had to call her and tell her he was coming over. That they had to talk it out. Work it out. That she didn't have to marry Akhil. That she *couldn't* marry Akhil. Because she didn't love Akhil, she loved him.

The fear of losing her to Akhil made him realize how much he loved her.

Love.

"Oh god." A wave of dizziness washed over him and he closed his eyes. Love. The one damn thing in this entire universe he didn't understand.

It had always eluded him. He'd thought at one time that love and passion were the same thing. That if you had the heat, you'd have the fire. But Ria had proved that wrong. And Tanya. He'd stirred up considerable heat with both of them, but it had died out. Not even ashes remained. After two big break-ups, he was not confident of getting into another relationship.

With Myra, it was different. There had been moments of passion, with enough heat to set the world aflame; but with her, there had been something else, something deep and profound and important.

Something he'd never really taken apart and looked at until now. A quiet thing. A solid, never-ending thing.

Love.

Slowly, very slowly, he eased out a tight breath he hadn't even known he'd been holding. He thought of it again, letting the word run through him.

The girl he loved was heading to marry Akhil.

With a sudden flash, he remembered Myra narrating to him a dialogue from one of her favourite movies *When Harry Met Sally*. "Somewhere out there is the man you are supposed to marry. And if you don't get him first, somebody else will, and you'll have to spend the rest of your life knowing that somebody else is married to your husband." Swearing breathlessly, he grabbed his car keys and was out the door in under two minutes, heart hammering against his ribs.

She would still be there, he told himself with forced calm as he accelerated and drove out.

He wouldn't be too late.

▼

Kairav stood at the door to Akhil's house. He pounded at the door. The servant opened the door and was about to ask him who he wanted, when Kairav just rushed inside the living room where he could see Myra sitting on the couch.

The servant ran behind Kairav, but Kairav entered the room and shut the door from inside.

"Myra, I need to talk to you," Kairav stood in the doorway, the calmness in his voice deceptive.

Myra went utterly motionless.

She stared at Kairav for a horrified moment. "What on earth—"

The silence stretched taut. Kairav stared across the room at Myra. She just sat there, staring back at him in astonishment. He looked terrible, his hair in disorder, face drooping down.

"What are you doing here Kairav?" Myra's voice was just a furious whisper.

"I am here to take you home," he assertively said.

"You can't just come in here and—" Myra caught herself. Drew in a deep breath. "Kairav, please leave. Now."

"No damn way you're mine. And I'm taking you back home. Now."

"Have you lost your mind?"

Myra opened her mouth, then closed it again, not having the faintest idea of what to say. He'd lost his mind, obviously. Maybe he was having the same kind of meltdown that she was.

"Myra, I don't even know where to start."

She looked at him more closely. He really was in bad shape.

"Kairav, would you like to sit down?" she asked gently. "How about a cup of coffee?" She gestured towards the Borosil carafe on the low centre table by the couch. "A drink?"

"I don't want to sit down, I don't want coffee, I don't want a drink. I want you. I *need* you." Slowly, as though half-afraid she'd bolt if he made a sudden move, he walked towards her. "You were right the other day when you said I couldn't see what was right in front of me. But it took damn near losing you to realize I love you. Probably always have."

"You love me?" She said it dryly, trying not to laugh. "Is this your idea of a joke, Kairav? Because it's not going to work. I am not coming back to work with you. Akhil and I are getting married, and—"

"I love you."

He said it almost rebelliously this time, jaw jutting forward slightly, as though daring her to deny it. Myra just looked at him, her mind a sudden blank.

"Well, damn it, aren't you going to say something?" He raked his hair back, looking exasperated and impatient, and started to pace. "I just didn't recognize it, that's all. I always figured love was... hell, passion. Fire. I didn't know it felt like a warm blanket. I didn't know what I've been feeling about you all this time was love."

"Kairav...Just stop it!" She was finding it difficult to breath. "Kairav," she repeated softly, "is this some sort of revenge thing? Are you telling me this now to get even with me for—"

"No, Myra." He walked across and put both hands on her shoulders, looking down into her eyes, serious and suddenly very calm. "I know you're in love with me. I know that. What I'm trying to explain is that I'm in love with you too. Not just that I love you, but I'm in love with you. There's a difference. I want you in my future."

Her eyes went wide. "You do?"

"I've tried to tell you several times over the past few days," he admitted. "But every time, we were either interrupted or you fell asleep on me. I want you forever, babe. Which means no more girlfriends. No more broken hearts. No more rebound lover. I want you exclusively."

She tried to smile, but out came a sob.

"I don't want you to marry Akhil, I want you to marry me. I want you to come back home and marry me and live with me. I want you in my life, Myra. Forever."

"Best friends?" Her voice broke slightly and she moved her finger on the scar on her thumb, gazed up at him, hardly even daring to believe.

"Husband and wife." He settled his mouth over hers, kissing her lightly. Evocatively.

The door behind them burst open. Kairav wheeled around, putting himself squarely between Myra and whoever was coming through.

Akhil stood there for a moment, eyes blazing. Then he gave a snort of laughter. "So it is you, Kairav. My servant thinks some thief has entered the house."

"I am," Kairav said bluntly.

Akhil nodded, a smile playing around his mouth. He was taller than Kairav remembered. And heavier through the chest.

"I wondered if you'd get here in time." The smile widened. "I was getting a little worried actually. If you hadn't turned up, I didn't know what the hell I was going to do. Marry Myra and keep my mouth shut, or do the honourable thing and come out to you to pound some sense into that thick skull of yours."

Myra gave a whiff of indignation and stepped around Kairav. "What do you mean you didn't know what you'd do? I thought you loved me!"

"I do, I really do," Akhil said gently. "Problem is, sweetheart, you don't love me."

"I most certainly do!"

Kairav nearly grinned. She sounded almost normal again.

"You love Kairav, not me. I've always known it, but I sort of hoped...well, it doesn't matter now."

Smiling, Akhil walked across and held out his hand. "You're a hell of a lucky man, Kairav. I just hope you know how lucky. Because if you screw up and hurt her, I'll—"

"I'm not going to screw up." Kairav took Akhil's hand and shook it firmly. "Not this time. This time, I have found the girl I love. And this time it's forever."

▼

A few months later

Love was in the air. It was a busy Sunday evening at Café Coffee Day, Dhaula Kuan. The café was bursting at the seams. Businessmen, housewives and families, all sipped their favourite blend. A few enjoyed gourmet bars and brownies, and desserts.

She entered the café, looked over the crowd, and searched out her husband. She found Kairav at a table against the far wall, sipping a black coffee, his cream puff untouched.

He looked up from a sports magazine, caught her staring, and winked. A sexy wink that always set her heart to beating faster. She loved this man.

The Info Capital deal had worked out great and had led to some exponential growth. UrbanFork was flourishing, with a great team and able leadership of the two directors.

They looked at each other and smiled broadly.

Life was good.

Kairav rose from his chair and crossed to where she stood. He leaned against the table, reaching out to slip his fingers around hers. The band of gold with studded diamonds on her ring finger glittered, and he ran his thumb over it wonderingly. Six months married, and he still couldn't believe it. And this time, he had no doubts at all that it was forever.

Myra tipped her face up to him and he smiled again, seeing that a blush had come into her cheeks.

"We still haven't come up with an idea for a wedding gift for Shruti and Sachin." Myra took a bite of the caramel roll he had ordered for her. "They're getting married in two weeks. I can't believe it."

"I can't believe I nearly let you get away from me," Kairav said quietly. "I can't believe I didn't see it. That I didn't know." He subdued a shudder, thinking of what his life could have been like if he hadn't gone after her.

"I can show you a website where we can buy really nice personalized gifts for their wedding. Can I use your laptop?"

"My laptop is your laptop."

"Same password?"

She'd finally caved in and told him her password – *LoveKairav*. It made him smile, that all these years, her password had been this.

And it had taken him so long to realize his love for her.

Now she was his. The girl he loved.